A MATCH
for Mischief

GAIL INGIS

GAIL INGIS

A MATCH FOR MISCHIEF

Copyright © 2025 by Gail Ingis

gailingis.com

Cover and book interior design and formatting:
Joanna D'Angelo

Copy Editor: Thomas Harrison Claus

Published in the United States of America Published by Ingis Design
Ideas

ISBN (Print) 978-1-7373369-9-0
ISBN (eBook) 978-1-7373369-8-3

A MATCH FOR MISCHIEF

A SWEET HISTORICAL ROMANCE FOR THE HOLIDAYS

THE AMERICAN HEIRESSES SERIES
BOOK THREE

GAIL INGIS

ACKNOWLEDGMENTS

To Joanna D'Angelo, my amazing editor, publicist, cover designer, friend, and confidant — thank you for your enthusiastic support, creativity, wisdom, and guidance. You challenge me to reach higher with every word, every line, and every page. My heartfelt thanks for shepherding this book to fruition. From editorial to marketing, publicity, art, and sales, to the beautiful design of the book cover — it's truly outstanding.

My heartfelt thanks to my fellow writers at CTRWA (Connecticut Romance Writers of America) for your friendship, inspiration, and endless encouragement. To our president, AK Nevermore, my deepest gratitude for your wisdom and guidance. Special thanks also to Diana Rock and Grace Hartwell, and to all the talented members whose names I may not have listed but whose support has meant so much.

To my wonderful family — my children, grandchildren, great-grandchildren and rumors have it, more branches are sprouting— your love, hugs, and lively texts fill my heart and keep me on my toes! You are my constant joy and inspiration.

And to my readers — thank you for spending time with my books, sharing your thoughts, and welcoming me as a friend. Your kindness and connection mean more than words can say.

DEDICATION

To my amazing husband, Tom —
my partner in mischief, my anchor,
and my biggest cheerleader.
You make every project an adventure,
and every day a joy.

CONTENTS

Chapter 1   1
A Winter's Tale at Baldwin Manor

Chapter 2   15
A Sparkling Vision

Chapter 3   23
An Open Heart

Chapter 4   31
An Enchanted Winter Waltz

Chapter 5   41
Mischief and Mistletoe

Chapter 6   53
A Kiss Before Midnight

Chapter 7   59
A Christmas Morning Promise

Chapter 8   69
A Romantic Wonderland

Chapter 9   79

Epilogue   85

Stories, Shenanigans & the Occasional
Cookie Recipe   93

FREE PREVIEW 1   95
The Memorable Mrs. Dempsey

FREE PREVIEW 2   107
The Unforgettable Miss Baldwin

About the Author   126

Books by Gail Ingis   129

CHAPTER 1

A WINTER'S TALE AT BALDWIN MANOR

NORWALK, CONNECTICUT ~ DECEMBER 6, 1888

*W*inter had arrived at Baldwin Manor in delicate silver spirals. Snow gathered like soft whispers on the tall windows of the east wing, where Mia Baldwin had her studio. Wiping her wet brush on a rag, she stepped back to contemplate her canvas. She'd been up since dawn, working to finish the painting—a portrait of her family she hoped would be her parents' Christmas gift.

A wisp of raven hair slipped free and tickled her cheek. Impatiently, she tucked it behind her ear and frowned at the canvas. Her blue eyes narrowed in concentration. Her petite, lithe frame moved gracefully

1

from easel to table as she added a touch of vermilion to her palette. She dipped her brush again, trying hard to ignore the memory of a voice that once questioned her color choices.

The vermilion stroke vexed her. Bold—perhaps too bold. And of course, she could still hear that voice— "Do you really think that little splash of vermilion belongs there?"

Robert McDougall.

Dr. McDougall.

Coroner McDougall.

Vineyard-owner McDougall.

The man had so many roles and so many opinions.

She huffed and dipped her brush anyway. He wasn't here. He was in Fairfield fussing over his vines, and she refused to let his long-ago critique guide her morning.

She'd met Robert over two years ago, when he, a forensic doctor with the Metropolitan Police Department, had helped solve a mystery for her sister, Allie. Mia remembered the day clearly—how she had accompanied Allie and Peter to Robert's home, how tense and strange that journey had been—before Allie and Peter had fallen in love, before they'd married, before happiness had softened the edges of their once-frequent quarrels.

At that first meeting, Mia had been surprised to see one of her own paintings on Robert's wall—one she'd sold to a lovely woman at an art show upstate. She would never forget the pain in Robert's eyes when she mentioned the buyer. What she hadn't known then was that the young woman had been Robert's wife... and that she had died.

Mia took a deep breath and let it out slowly. Dr. Robert McDougall had lodged himself in her thoughts far more persistently than she liked to admit. Life was busy enough to keep him in the shadows of her mind but whenever she was unsure of a brushstroke, a texture, a color—his memory stepped forward, uninvited and unhelpfully opinionated.

The canvas glowed in the crisp north light. Every color demanded precision. Every unspoken emotion tugged at her.

Painting was her passion, and her studio was her sanctuary. The only place where no one pried, no one pushed, no one told her she must hurry up and marry, and absolutely no one called a carefully placed stroke of vermilion "pretty."

Her eyes narrowed again.

Pretty.

Artists despised that word. Pretty was for hats, not art.

At last, Mia set her brush down and stretched— time for a break.

A few minutes later, she curled up in her favorite

armchair in the adjoining library. The velvet chairs clustered companionably around a cheerful fire, and the rows of books rose before her like familiar, welcoming faces. Little by little, the tension eased from her shoulders; the hush of the room settled over her like a soft shawl.

Mia lifted her teacup, letting the warm steam brush her cheek before taking a slow, steadying sip. Only then, with a soft sigh, did she reach for her well-worn copy of *Jane Eyre*.

She'd read the novel so many times the pages fell open on their own—always to the moment Jane chose self-respect over love. It was heartbreaking, but Mia admired Jane's integrity, her quiet strength.

Mia soon lost herself in the book as snow muffled the world, granting a brief reprieve from Aunt Cornelia's relentless matchmaking schemes and society's constant insistence that Mia was well past due to marry.

Percy, her sweet Dalmatian puppy, awoke from his pillow in front of the fire and padded toward her, knocking a stack of her father's newspaper proofs to the floor with one exuberant thump. "Oh, you're lucky Papa is in the city, Percy," Mia murmured as she bent to straighten the pile. Her father was in New York for meetings at the *New York Sentinel* with Adam and John

—her brothers, the latter adopted but every bit as beloved.

The pup tilted his adorable spotted head and gave a soft, apologetic *woof*, which clearly meant, "Forgive me and give me a biscuit."

"Percy," Mia sighed, trying—and failing—to sound stern as a smile tugged at her lips at her cheeky pup.

Nearby, her sister Emma's African Grey parrot, Lord Wilby, mirrored the dog's tilt from atop his gilded perch.

"PERCY! PERCY!" he squawked in Mia's exact tone.

Emma and twin Ava were also in New York for two days, Christmas shopping with terrifying efficiency, so naturally Lord Wilby had appointed himself Mia's supervisor until their return. He refused to be left alone with "only boring humans," as Emma liked to say.

"All right, Lord Wilby, we know how brilliant you are."

"BRILLIANT! BRILLIANT!" he proclaimed, feathers puffed with theatrical pride. Emma had taught him the word last summer, and Wilby had used it at every possible—and impossible—opportunity ever since.

Mia smiled, breaking off a small bit of the lemon and vanilla cookie on her plate and handing it to Percy. The Dalmatian sighed in bliss, curled at her feet, and promptly drifted into snoring slumber while Lord

Wilby muttered, "BRILLIANT," under his breath like a scholar agreeing with himself.

With a chuckle, Mia picked up *Jane Eyre* again.

Helen, her maid, arrived a few minutes later carrying a small kettle of hot water and the expression of someone bearing headlines hot off the press. She refreshed Mia's teapot with practiced efficiency before leaning in, her voice dropping to a conspiratorial whisper.

"They've begun, miss. Your mother and Mrs. Bigelow. The Christmas Ball menu." She straightened, adopting the gravity of a battlefield correspondent. "Mrs. Bigelow has just declared there is *absolutely not enough cinnamon*."

"Every year," Mia said with a wry chuckle.

Helen nodded sagely. "Tradition, miss. Some households pass down silverware; we pass down kitchen skirmishes."

The maid retreated with a sympathetic smile, and Mia took another sip of tea, grateful her mother had the good sense to keep Mrs. Bigelow, the cook, and Mrs. Whitcombe, the housekeeper, stationed at opposite ends of the house during holiday preparations. The two women were usually the closest of allies, but at this time of year even their steadfast friendship showed a few hairline cracks—the natural consequence of trying to organize the Baldwin estate into festive order.

At this very moment, Mrs. Whitcombe was commanding an entire battalion of maids and footmen as they readied the ballroom. Windows were scrubbed until they winked in the afternoon light; polished brass gleamed like captured starlight; and the parquet floor was buffed to within an inch of surrender. Every year, the housekeeper delivered the same ironclad decree: "If the chandeliers do not blind me upon entry, then they are not polished enough."

Between cleaning, baking, polishing, planning, and the general Baldwin enthusiasm for Christmas, Mia was fortunate to find even a half-hour of solitude.

She nestled deeper into her armchair, book balanced on her knee, firelight dancing across the pages.

And for that precious moment—everything was warm, still, and perfectly peaceful.

Then—

The library doors flung open, and a burst of cool air swept through the library.

And a figure flew in like a cannonball wrapped in velvet.

"Darling Mia!" Aunt Cornelia trilled. "You must meet Mr. Tennyson—exquisite breeding, recently returned from Italy, a poet and a musician of the highest order! The man has so many gifts!"

Mia calmly turned a page of *Jane Eyre*. "How

delightful. Perhaps he'll strum something uplifting while I leap off the balcony for dramatic effect."

"Mia! Must you always be so outrageous? You are two-and-twenty! You'll be a spinster if you're not careful!"

"Oh dear," Mia murmured. "Shall I start choosing my cats for company?"

Aunt Cornelia huffed, shot a warning glare at Lord Wilby, who squawked "OH DEAR! OH DEAR!" then swept dramatically toward the doorway to usher in Mr. Tennyson himself. No surprise there. He was moony-eyed, dreamy-faced, and clutching a lute as though he'd rescued it from pirates on the high seas.

Without invitation, he launched straight into a sonnet."Your eyes, dear lady, glimmer like two lanterns in the fog of my despair..."

Please let the fog swallow me instead, Mia thought.

"My heart crumbles like a fragile biscuit whenever you look my way!"

Mia calmly took a bite of her biscuit. If anyone's heart were to crumble, she preferred it to be made of flour and sugar.

"Oh my, such raw, unfiltered talent," Aunt Cornelia breathed, one hand pressed dramatically to her chest. "I am moved to tears."

"I am moved to tears, but for a different reason," Mia muttered under her breath. Poor man, to share a name with the great Tennyson and possess none of the talent.

She lifted a silent prayer toward the heavens.

Might rescue arrive... immediately?

It arrived, but not in the way she'd envisioned.

Barnes, the butler, cleared his throat. "Miss Baldwin, a gentleman wishes to see you. Dr. Robert McDougall."

Mia nearly dropped her book.

Robert? Here?

Heaven help her—she'd just been thinking about him.

Cornelia pounced. "Mia! Who is Dr. Robert McDougall? Why does that name sound so familiar?"

"An acquaintance," Mia said more sharply than she'd intended. "You met him at Allie and Peter's wedding, remember?" Aunt Cornelia was bothersome, but she was her mother's sister. "A doctor. A detective. A coroner. And the owner of a vineyard in Fairfield, Connecticut. Barnes, please send him in."

Robert entered like a gust of winter wind—tall, broad-shouldered, smelling faintly of cedar and cold air. And behind the composed exterior, his hazel eyes reminded her of golden amber in the light. Oh Lord, next thing she'd be reciting a sonnet worse than Tennyson's. He always seemed to unsettle her. She didn't understand why... Well, that wasn't quite true.

Everything about him spoke of passion—bold and fierce—held in check. For some silly schoolgirl reason, he reminded her of Mr. Rochester.

A chance meeting at the Metropolitan Museum of Art a few months ago had quite surprised her. And that was putting it mildly.

She'd turned and there he was, standing not three feet away in front of a painting she adored.

"It's overworked," he'd said curtly. "The artist didn't know when to stop."

Mia, scandalized, had replied, "I like its vibrancy."

Robert had made the fatal mistake. "It's... pretty."

Pretty.

She'd wanted to whack him with her museum guide.

And to make matters worse, a guard had cleared his throat like a disapproving bullfrog, forcing her to step back. "Yes, yes, don't breathe on the Rembrandt," she'd muttered. She had positioned herself without thinking, too close to the painting—no doubt as a protective gesture against Robert's criticism.

Behind her, a gaggle of schoolchildren had thundered through, shouting questions about statues and painting colors as if the quiet gallery were a playground. And just as she was recovering her dignity from the guard's reprimand, a patron with a massive pink hat had approached.

"Excuse me, dear, where are the *Water Lilies*?"

"I'm sorry, but I don't work here," Mia had replied.

"Oh. Well, you look like you know things."

"I try not to make a habit of it," she'd quipped quietly.

Robert, standing beside her, had raised a dark eyebrow, seemingly in amusement.

The memory made her lips twitch. Even now. Now, when he'd once again blown into her life, her home, casting that same steady gaze across the library, at her.

He acknowledged Cornelia and the musician/poet with a brief nod. "Pardon me for intruding."

"It's quite all right," Mia said as she got up from her chair. She quickly made the introductions and reintroductions for Aunt Cornelia. The older woman almost swooned. The musician/poet looked like he was about to burst into tears.

"A doctor! A detective! And a vineyard! How perfect!"

Mia clenched her teeth…"Aunt Cornelia!" she warned.

"Ta-ta, darling!" Cornelia said, dragging the bereft musician/poet along with her.

The parrot squawked, "TA-TA! DARLING!"

"Miss Baldwin," Robert said, bowing over her hand, voice deep and controlled. "Forgive the intrusion, but I would appreciate a word."

Mia gestured toward the adjoining door to the studio.

Percy, now up, regarded them with a curious look on his face. Mia chuckled as she introduced her dog, a gift from Allie and Peter on her last birthday. And, of course, Lord Wilby, whom Robert already knew.

Robert's lips curved up in a smile as the parrot rode Percy's back into the studio. "Do you always bring such energy with you?"

"Only on Tuesdays," she said sweetly, grinning.

Back in the studio, sunlight pooled across her paints. Mia reached for her brush, dipping once more into the vermilion.

Robert watched. "You are still using that color."

"And?"

"It's... again... very—"

She turned her head slowly. "Say it, Robert."

"Pretty?"

The parrot squawked, "PRETTY! PRETTY!" in triumph.

Robert raised his brows. Mia sighed. Percy barked.

It was chaos, and Robert stood in the middle of it stoically, like a general going into battle.

Finally, he cleared his throat. "I need your help. With the opening of my winery."

"You do?" she said, both surprised and intrigued.

"You see truth, Mia. You paint what most people

miss. I would like you to design my wine label and paint a mural for the tasting room. I want art to reflect what I am building there."

She blinked. "You believe art can do that?"

"I believe you can do that."

Mia fixed her attention on him, as if seeing him anew. There, behind his steady composure, was a wound that time had still not healed. "I think there is more you are not saying."

His jaw tightened. "I once worked to keep people alive, and now I keep vines alive. At least they don't look to me for miracles."

Mia stepped closer, her heart stirring despite herself. His eyes held hers and she almost lost herself in their depths.

She set her brush down on the table next to her easel. "Art can't heal the past. But perhaps it can brighten the future."

He met her gaze, something tender flickering behind his eyes. He studied her for a long moment, the corners of his mouth curving up into a slight smile. "That's exactly what I hoped you'd say."

CHAPTER 2

A SPARKLING VISION

FAIRFIELD, CONNECTICUT ~ DECEMBER 8, 1888

Mia stepped down from the train, the crisp December air rushing to greet her the moment her boots touched the platform. Sunlight glittered along the rails, turning frost into flecks of diamond dust. Percy gave a delighted bark, tugging at his leash as if the world itself were calling him forward.

"Stay close, Percy," Mia murmured, though her own heart thudded with just as much eagerness as the puppy's. Robert had been entirely serious when he invited her to visit his estate and winery. And Mia—

impulsively, boldly—had suggested sooner rather than later.

She'd begged her mother to come as chaperone, half-expecting Clara to point out the chaos waiting at home: the looming Baldwin Christmas Ball, the never-ending holiday preparations, the thousand small tasks that needed her attention.

But Mia had cleverly added that after visiting the winery, they could stop by Allie and Peter's home to spend time with the twins, only a stone's throw from Robert's property.

That had done the trick.

Clara agreed, with a sigh that sounded suspiciously like fond resignation.

And now here they were—Mia, her mother, and an excited Dalmatian—stepping into a day she'd scarcely dared hope for.

Clara descended behind her with the porter's assistance, lowering her veil as a breeze swept across the small Fairfield station. The town was quieter than Norwalk, framed by rolling hills and stretches of winter fields dusted with silver.

And there—standing beside a dark green carriage —was Robert.

He stood tall in his wool overcoat, his gloved hands by his side. The morning sun caught the warm tones in his hair and sparked gold in his hazel eyes. The corners of his mouth curved into a smile, so open, so unexpectedly bright that Mia's breath tangled somewhere between her lungs and her corset stays.

He looks... different.

Lighter somehow.

Younger, even.

How and when had that happened?

"Mrs. Baldwin. Miss. Baldwin. Welcome." He bowed with that quiet dignity that always seemed part of him. But his gaze lingered on Mia a half-second longer... intent, almost searching.

Oh, goodness, those butterflies were doing somersaults in her stomach again.

"Robert," Clara greeted warmly. "Thank you for meeting us so early."

"It is my pleasure," he said, taking Clara's hand, then turning to Mia. "I hope your journey was a comfortable one."

"It was," Mia said, hoping her voice didn't betray the entirely inconvenient swoop in her stomach. "And Percy enjoyed his first train ride immensely."

At the sound of his name, Percy leaped up, paws flailing, tail wagging so hard Mia feared he might launch into flight. Robert chuckled, a deep, rich sound that brushed over her like velvet.

"Good morning, Percy," he said, rubbing the puppy's head. Percy promptly attempted to lick his glove

"Well," Clara said, amused, "it appears Robert has passed Percy's inspection."

Mia swallowed a smile as Robert helped them into the carriage. The moment he climbed in opposite her, the space shrunk. She caught the faint scent of cedar and cold winter air on his coat, and tried—unsuccessfully—not to admire how tall and broad-shouldered he was.

Two days ago, he'd appeared at Baldwin Manor as if the past two years had not stretched between them like a long, silent road. Well, except for that unexpected encounter at the Metropolitan Museum a few months ago. A meeting that had unsettled her and lingered in her thoughts far longer than she'd ever admit aloud.

And now here he was again... smiling. Inviting.

Different.

Or perhaps she was the one who felt different— more aware of him, more curious, more drawn to him than she had any right to be. She was no closer to understanding it than she had been the moment he walked into the library at Baldwin Manor.

The carriage wheels rolled smoothly over the countryside road, the landscape spreading into sloping fields and quiet clusters of winter trees. Clara made pleasant conversation, asking after Robert's mother's health, the progress of the vineyard, and whether he had decorated for Christmas.

He answered each question graciously, but Mia sensed his attention slipping toward her between every sentence, as though he were studying her reactions—the way she smiled, the way she tugged absently at her glove, the way Percy kept pawing at her skirts.

Her cheeks heated. She pretended not to notice. But it was oh so difficult not to feel every single glance warming her from head to toe.

When the carriage turned onto a private drive, Mia drew in a quiet breath. The McDougall home came into view—a gracious, stone-and-shingle manor nestled against a rise in the land. Smoke drifted from two chimneys. Frost glimmered along the verandah railings. It was not as large or imposing as Baldwin Manor, but it was warm, inviting, beautifully kept, and undeniably charming.

"Oh, Robert," Clara said. "What a lovely home."

His eyes glowed with quiet pride. "Thank you. It has been a great deal of work, but it feels worth it."

They stepped inside, and Percy exploded with joy—sniffing corners, prancing across rugs, greeting the house as if it had been built solely for him. Mia laughed and apologized, but Robert smiled and said, "He's welcome."

The entry hall was bright with pale winter light. The sitting room held a graceful arrangement of comfortable chairs, shelves lined with books, and a large stone hearth already crackling with a morning fire. Clara inspected a vase of winter greenery with an approving nod.

"It suits you perfectly," Mia said.

"It suits the life I wish to build," he replied, his gaze meeting Mia's, making her breath catch.

He showed them the dining room, the solarium, the modest but lovely music room, and finally his small study. Each room felt... lived in. Tended. Hopeful.

"Now," Robert said, buttoning his coat, "if you are ready, the winery is only a short drive from here."

The vineyard sprawled across the hillside in long, orderly rows—bare vines in winter slumber, yet even in their stark state, Mia felt the promise of what they would become under the spring sun.

The winery building itself was a handsome brick structure with tall windows and a pitched roof trimmed with dark wood. Inside, the cool air held the clean scents of oak, earth, and fermenting fruit.

Robert walked with them through the workroom— large presses, racks of barrels, bottle storage, and narrow vents that let in winter air for temperature regulation.

Mia touched a smooth oak barrel, admiring its craftsmanship. "It feels... alive," she murmured without thinking.

Robert glanced at her, a tender flicker in those hazel

depths. They passed into the unfinished tasting room—a high-ceilinged space with tall windows overlooking the vineyard.

"This," Robert said, gesturing around them, "is where I hope the mural might go. I imagine this wall would be best suited for it." He tapped a spacious expanse of smooth plaster.

Mia stepped closer, envisioning the possibilities.

Warm colors. Flowing lines. A story of the land from root to fruit.

She traced the air with her hand.

"You could anchor it with the house," she said. "At sunrise. Vines stretching outward. A sense of growth... of life... of legacy."

Robert's breath eased out slowly, as though her words had struck something profound.

"Yes," he said. "Exactly, yes."

Then, with a smile that sent heat coursing through her, he added, "You always see the heart of things, Mia."

Her stomach fluttered—light and foolish and wonderful.

Clara clasped her hands. "This is extraordinarily forward-thinking, Robert. A tasting room, events... perhaps, even weddings someday."

Robert chuckled. "Possibly. Eventually, I hope to build a country inn. An elegant restaurant as well, featuring seasonal dishes infused with our wines. But that will be years yet."

"You've thought of everything," Clara said, visibly impressed.

"I had good teachers," he replied. "Joseph. Rork. Peter. And a hotelier friend of theirs—Mr. Winslow."

Clara laughed. "Ah, yes. I should have known. That man cannot resist a new venture."

"Speaking of ventures," Robert added, "Mrs. Drummond, my cook, has prepared a light luncheon for us back at the house. She's included a young white wine, on which I would value your thoughts."

Percy barked enthusiastically, as if volunteering his opinion as well.

Robert smiled.

Mia did too.

And something new and hopeful settled between them.

CHAPTER 3

AN OPEN HEART

FAIRFIELD, CONNECTICUT ~ DECEMBER 9, 1888

*T*he morning air was sharp and clean, the kind that woke a man straight to the marrow. Frost clung to the vineyard posts, turning each wooden beam into a silver pillar beneath the pale winter sun. Robert set his shoulder to the weight of a crate, lifting it onto the wagon with more force than was needed. Physical labor steadied him, kept thoughts from spiraling into places he wasn't ready to face. Or rather... thoughts of one person.

Mia.

It had always been there—ever since he'd first met

her—humming quietly beneath the surface. But it had truly sparked last spring at the Metropolitan Museum of Art. That unexpected encounter. That moment when he realized it was Mia standing a mere few feet away looking at the same painting he'd been quietly criticizing under his breath.

He'd been in New York to meet with Mr. Winslow, the hotelier investing in the winery, and had stopped into the museum afterward to pass an hour before his train. The galleries were warm with sunlight then, full of students and tourists.

And there she was.

The way she had defended the painting—her chin lifting, blue eyes flashing with intelligence and conviction—stirred something in him he hadn't felt in years. She seemed to brighten the very light in the gallery, as though she carried a quiet, unmistakable radiance of her own.

After that day, he hadn't been able to push her from his mind.

Not through the harvest.

Not through the long nights planning the bottling schedule.

Not through meetings with investors. He kept searching for a way to invite her into that future—genuinely, respectfully, without daring too much. And then the idea came.

Natural.

Obvious.

Perfect.

Her artistry. Her vision. Her uncanny ability to see the soul where others saw only structure.

Commissioning her to design the wine label and paint a mural hadn't been a convenient excuse. It had been the truth. The vineyard needed her creative spirit.

And his life... well, he was beginning to understand that he needed her, too.

Her eyes—those luminous sapphire eyes—seemed to see straight into him, past every defense he'd built. And for the first time in years, the idea of letting someone see that deeply didn't unsettle him.

It felt like hope.

He wiped an arm across his brow and bent for another crate.

"I see you've taken up a second career as a field hand," came a familiar voice.

Robert straightened. Peter Harrison strode down the path between the rows, a relaxed confidence in every step. Snow clung to the tops of his boots. He had turned up his coat collar against the wind. Behind him, Robert's foreman, Mr. Dugan, gave a respectful nod and retreated toward the work sheds.

"Morning, Peter," Robert said, shifting the crate onto the wagon. "Didn't expect to see you this early."

"I just came from escorting Clara and Mia to the station."Peter leaned against a fence post. "Thought I'd stop by on my way home to check on you."

Robert paused. Check on him? What was that supposed to mean?

Peter crossed his arms, staring out at the winter horizon as if weighing a possibility in the quiet distance. "You've built quite a place," he said. "Takes a man with determination. Or a man trying to outrun his past."

Robert frowned. "If you came here to analyze me, you should have brought your notebook and spectacles."

Peter laughed. "I left those in New York. Today I'm simply a friend."

Robert didn't respond. He reached for another crate instead.

Peter watched him for another long moment. "So... Mia told Allie you asked her for artistic help."

Robert's grip tightened on the wooden handle of the crate. "Yes. She has talent. Real talent."

"Mmm." Peter's voice held far too much amusement. "Talent. That's what you're calling it."

Robert shot him a warning look.

But Peter only grinned. "I know you had other options. Rork, for instance. He's one of your investors. A renowned artist. An obvious choice."

"I don't need Rork," Robert murmured, adjusting the wagon's harness. "I asked Mia because—because—" He stopped. Because why? Because her art moved him? Because the way she spoke about light and color made him think about his life? Because her presence made the darkness he'd lived in for so long less suffocating? He didn't know how to say any of that to Peter. He'd never been good at sharing his feelings with anyone, let alone another man.

Peter's smile faded. "Robert. I'm not trying to pry. I'm trying to understand. Mia's like a sister to me. Her heart is—"

"Tender," Robert finished quietly. "I know."

He placed another crate onto the wagon and braced his palms on the wagon's edge. The cold air stung his lungs as he inhaled. He slowly blew out a deep breath. "I would never hurt her."

Peter shook his head. "That's not what I'm suggesting. But unless your intentions are serious and earnest, I would ask you to tread carefully."

Robert swung around sharply. "You think I'm toying with her?"

"No." Peter laid a gloved hand on the side of the wagon. "But I think you're afraid to admit what you want."

Silence settled between them, broken only by the distant chatter of workers and the clink of tools.

27

Robert looked out over the vineyard—the neat winter rows, trellis posts standing like sentinels, and the burlap-and-straw-wrapped vines resting beneath their mounds of hilled earth. They looked almost peaceful in their winter coats, waiting for spring to wake them.

"Do you know why I built this place?" he asked quietly.

Peter didn't answer, allowing him space.

"I could have gone back to private practice," Robert continued. "Or stayed with the Metropolitan Police. God knows they begged me to. But I couldn't..." His voice caught, roughened. "I was drowning in death, in darkness. I needed something—anything—alive."

Peter stood still.

"So, I bought land," Robert said, voice steadier. "Stubborn, unforgiving land. And I started digging. Planting. Pruning. Learning. It gave me a purpose again." He hesitated. "And when Mia looked at the vines yesterday... it felt like she understood what I've been trying to build."

"A home?" Peter asked.

"A legacy," Robert corrected. "A creation that endures. One anchored to the land." His throat tightened and he looked directly into Peter's eyes. "Mia is the only woman I can imagine sharing it with."

For the first time that morning, Peter's expression

softened completely. "Well," he said, clapping Robert on the shoulder, "that answers my question."

Robert let out a slow, almost disbelieving exhale. Saying it aloud had felt like prying open a rusted lock in his chest.

Peter helped Robert lift the last crate onto the wagon and secure the strap. "Are you coming to the Baldwin Christmas Ball next week?"

"I received the invitation," Robert said, rubbing the back of his neck. "Wasn't sure if I would attend."

"Maybe you should think about it."

Robert arched a brow. "You're suggesting I go?"

"If your intentions are true?" Peter said. "Then yes. Go."

The winter breeze swept through the vineyard, carrying the faint scent of pine from the distant woods. He looked out over the land he had fought to cultivate, the land that now hummed with possibility.

Yes. Maybe he would go. Maybe it was time.

Peter tipped his hat. "Good. Then I'll see you there."

As he walked away, a sudden awareness stirred inside him—not fear, not doubt. A ray of hope. An open heart. At last.

CHAPTER 4

AN ENCHANTED WINTER WALTZ

NORWALK, CONNECTICUT ~ DECEMBER 15, 1888

he ballroom at Baldwin Manor glimmered with soft golden candlelight from ornate sconces with tall, tapered candles. Gas-lit crystal chandeliers scattered reflections across polished floors and gilded mirrors. The crisp, fresh scent of pine from festive boughs lining the doorways and staircases mingled with the smoky sweetness of roasted chestnuts. Outside, snow fell lightly, coating the grounds in quiet silver—a perfect complement to the warmth and laughter within.

Guests arrived through the porte-cochère, their

laughter spilling into the hall as they were greeted with familiar warmth by Clara and Joseph Baldwin. Baldwin Manor's Annual Christmas Ball, long regarded as one of the Holiday Season's most elegant gatherings, hummed with anticipation. Music drifted from the orchestra—a lilting waltz carried across the room, violins and cello weaving a melodious tapestry of sound. Gentlemen in tailcoats and ladies in silken gowns moved gracefully across the parquet, punctuated by laughter and lively conversation.

Mia and Allie entered together, their gowns whispering across the floor. Allie's cranberry silk caught the light, gleaming like polished garnet, while Mia's deep blue satin shimmered like winter twilight. Heads turned as they passed through the doorway—acquaintances pressed forward to exchange greetings.

Mia glanced around the ballroom, seeing her twin sisters, Ava and Emma, chatting animatedly with their friends. Standing by the window, Aunt Cornelia was in deep conversation with the widow, Mrs. Caldecott. *Oh, dear.* Mia hoped her aunt wasn't inquiring about Mrs. Caldecott's bachelor son, Walter. The man was nearly 40! And, goodness, he was shorter than Mia.

"I think I would have rather curled up with my sweet Amy and Noah," Allie whispered as they walked up to the refreshment table.

"I would have stayed with you," Mia said with a

smile. "We could have read Mr. Dickens' *A Christmas Carol.*"

"Tomorrow. We'll have a nice, quiet evening," Allie said as she handed Mia a cup of eggnog. Allie had just finished reading *'Twas the Night Before Christmas* by Clement Clarke Moore to her babies. Ten months old, the two cherubs gazed adoringly at their mother as she acted out the story. They finally fell asleep, no doubt dreaming of dancing sugar plums.

"How is your painting coming along for the fundraiser?" Allie asked, looping her arm through Mia's as they stepped away from the refreshment table.

"Well, I'm nearly finished," Mia said. "It's a winter view of Central Park—fresh snow along the Bow bridges, the lake glazed with ice, and the street lamps casting a golden glow across the drifts. I wanted a serene scene, but magical."

"Oh, that will fetch a handsome sum for the suffragette cause," Allie nodded. "A landscape like that will charm donors into loosening their purse strings."

"I hope it will for such an important cause," Mia said. "Speaking of which, how goes your correspondence with Mrs. Julia Ward Howe? Do you think she'll agree to give a short address?"

"I'm encouraged," Allie replied. "She wrote that she hopes to attend and would be pleased to speak. Can you imagine? Julia Ward Howe lending her voice to our fundraiser? The Republic's Daughters would gain instant gravitas. And if Clara Louise Kellogg agrees to perform—well—between Mrs. Kellogg's voice and Mrs. Howe's words, even the most indifferent guests might donate with enthusiasm."

"We should send personal invitations to key supporters," Mia said. "Local leaders, prominent families, businessmen willing to contribute funds or services."

"Already underway," Allie said. "Papa is donating, of course—advertisements in *The New York Sentinel* and *The Chicago Gazette*."

"And Johnny and Adam's articles?" Mia asked. Their foster brother Johnny was their father's right hand at the *Sentinel* and their older brother Adam ran the *Gazette*. Both brothers had proven themselves to be just as brilliant and successful, as their prominent father. Mia missed them both. Neither could make it in time for the ball but would be arriving soon to spend the Holidays with the family.

"Hopefully we'll raise enough funds to support the publication of pamphlets, lecture tours, training volunteers—everything the movement needs for the coming year," Mia said.

"Exactly. Imagine it, Mia—one day women may actually win the vote."

"Yes," Mia breathed. "Perhaps in our lifetimes."

Allie smoothed her skirt. "If not ours, then our children."

"Speak for yourself," Mia said, lifting a brow. "You've got a head start. I'm not even married."

Allie shot her a sly look. "Oh, I have a suspicion that will change sooner than you think."

"And how do you imagine that will happen?" Mia quipped. "Is Prince Charming going to stride into the ballroom tonight and sweep me into a waltz?"

"Well, it is Christmastime," Allie said, eyes dancing. "A season when anything is possible."

A tall silver candelabra, its branches lifted like a frozen tree in bloom, anchored the refreshment table draped in silvery silk cloth. Cascading white roses and trailing ivy framed the flickering candles, and the surrounding crystal votives glittered like scattered stars across fresh snow.

Just as they leaned in to admire the decorations, a sudden thump-thump-thump shook the parquet. Captyn, Allie's Great Dane, loped into the ballroom, tail wagging like a small flag. He nudged a chair with his enormous head, sending it sliding across the floor, and the candelabra teetered precariously.

"Captyn!" Peter exclaimed, rushing in through the open French doors that led to the garden. Lunging for the dog's collar, he turned to regard his wife, who smiled in understanding.

"Forgive me, darling," Peter kissed Allie's cheek as he reined in the white and black spotted dog. "I was out with a few of the fellows, enjoying a cigar. Captyn was playing in the snow when he suddenly took off and made a beeline for the ballroom."

The dog, thinking it a new game, spun in a circle, knocking over a tray of hors d'oeuvres. Guests gasped, then laughed, the brief chaos adding an unexpected entertainment to the evening.

Allie bent and whispered something to Captyn, who gave a deep *woof* in reply and obediently heeled beside Peter. "He should be fine now, darling."

"Have I told you lately how amazing you are?"

"Oh, many times, but I never get tired of hearing it. Come, I'll help you get this overgrown pup settled in for the night. We'll be back soon," Allie said over her shoulder to Mia as they escorted Captyn from the ballroom.

Mia sighed inwardly at the tender glow that radiated between Allie and Peter. When they first met, they had their differences. But love had found its way. A love so bright it could light up a winter night. A muted ache rose in Mia's chest. She wanted that kind of connection, that kind of certainty. Someone who looked at her the way Peter looked at Allie.

She lifted her eggnog for another sip, letting the sweetness soothe her, as her gaze drifted across the ballroom. That was when she saw him—tall, impeccably dressed—greeting her parents with the familiar respectful inclination of his head.

Robert.

He looked up as if he'd somehow sensed her watching. Their eyes met across the room—those eyes that never failed to steal her breath. Her heart executed a neat somersault, exactly on cue.

"Mia," he said a moment later, his deep baritone curling deliciously through the festive din as he approached. "You've outshone the crystal chandeliers."

Heat fluttered across her cheeks. She brushed back a strand of hair, willing her smile to remain composed. "Only because the candles have decided to be flattering tonight. I'm surprised to see you. I didn't think you had an interest in grand social events."

"People can change," he said, and the slow curve of his smile gave her a feeling that the evening might change as well.

Oh goodness. He was even more handsome when he smiled—dangerously so. "I was mulling a few ideas for the wine label and mural," Mia managed, hoping her voice sounded steadier to him than to her own ears.

"I'd love to hear them," he said. "But first... would you do me the honor of a dance?"

As if on cue, the opening strains of *The Blue Danube*

floated through the ballroom—one of her requests. The melody unfurled like a ribbon of winter light.

"Yes," she breathed. "That would be wonderful."

Robert swept her onto the dance floor, his hand firm and reassuring at her waist, guiding her into the rythmic flow of the waltz. The other couples blurred into motion around them, silk and satin gliding beneath the crystal chandeliers.

Mia enjoyed the dance, and for one dizzying, perfect moment, she knew she was exactly where she wanted to be.

Robert led Mia around the dance floor to the strains of the waltz, knowing he was precisely where he wanted to be. Nothing could have stopped him from coming tonight. Mia was vibrant and beautiful, and spending time with her had begun to thaw his frozen heart.

He couldn't move forward with one foot still in the past. It was time to face his future.

Buying the property and creating a winery had been a way for him to work through his grief. And now, two years later, those vines he'd tended had finally rewarded him—pale-gold clusters pressed into a bright, sparkling white, and deep burgundy grapes ripened into a bold young red. As snow had drifted over the hills of his growing estate, he knew he was ready—not just to show Mia what he'd built, but to win her heart.

Around them, the ballroom continued its swirl of color, music, and light, glittering against the dark winter night. Snow settled on Baldwin Manor, a serene reminder that while the world rested, dreams and plans were already shaping the future.

CHAPTER 5

MISCHIEF AND MISTLETOE

NORWALK, CONNECTICUT ~ CHRISTMAS EVE, 1888

*N*ine days had passed since the Christmas ball—nine days in which Mia had replayed a certain waltz far more times than she would ever confess aloud.

And now, on this bright, still morning, Baldwin Manor was lively once more as the rest of the family arrived for the Holidays.

Uncle Rork and Aunt Leila had swept in with their entire brood the day before. Leila and Clara were dear friends from childhood, and their children had grown up like cousins. Rork and Leila's son, Liam, and his wife,

Margaret, were there with their three little girls, Eleanor, Josephine, and Betsy. Liam's sister, Beatrice, was also there. She was closest to Mia in age, unmarried, and blissfully unaware that Aunt Cornelia had likely marked her as her next matchmaking "project."

"Do you mean Aunt Cornelia actually brought that musician to the house for you to meet?" Bea asked as they strolled along the snow-covered grounds.

"Yes," Mia aimed her eyes at the heavens for patience. "And he seemed quite disconsolate when I didn't swoon at his impromptu sonnet."

"Oh dear. She truly is determined." Bea shook her head, her golden curls bouncing as her bright green eyes sparkled with amusement.

"Which is precisely why I'm warning you," Mia said. "You may be next."

"Goodness! Well, if a wandering poet emerges from behind a potted fern clutching a mandolin, I'll assume Aunt Cornelia had a hand in it," Bea laughed.

Mia couldn't contain her own mirth, their laughter fit together just as it always had—two friends sharing the same wry sense of humor. But even with Bea beside her, warm and familiar as ever, Mia kept one thought tucked quietly inside her heart. She didn't mention Robert's unexpected arrival at the house, nor the trip to the vineyard, nor their waltz at the ball... the one she could still feel in her bones when she closed her eyes.

It wasn't that she didn't trust Bea. She didn't yet know what to make of Robert. Or of the way her heart had seemed to rearrange itself the moment he'd taken her hand.

It had surprised her to see him at the Christmas ball —Robert McDougall did not make a habit of attending social gatherings. And she had been even more surprised when he'd sought her out and asked her to dance. And yes, it was unforgettable.

She knew her parents had invited him for Christmas, but whether he would actually come—well, that remained uncertain. And judging by the butterflies fluttering restlessly in her stomach, she cared far more than she ought.

"How is your novel coming along?" Mia asked, grasping at a safer subject before her thoughts tied themselves in knots.

"Well, I'm working on the second half," Bea said. "But I've reached a troublesome point. I can't decide how my hero should admit he's in love with my heroine."

Mia looped her arm through Bea's as they crossed a bumpy patch of path. "Why not have your heroine say it first? A bold twist—and exactly the nudge your stoic hero might need."

Bea blinked, then laughed. "I never thought of that! But it suits them perfectly. Thank you, Mia."

"Don't thank me," Mia giggled. "You're the talented writer. Those first chapters you sent were enchanting—I can't wait to see where the story goes."

Bea squeezed Mia's hand. "I appreciate your faith in me. And speaking of talent," Bea said, "Allie told me about your painting for the suffragette fundraiser. It sounds beautiful."

Mia pushed a stubborn curl behind her ear. "Oh, I hope people agree. Will you be attending?"

"Yes, we all will. Mother and Father are looking forward to it. And Father said he wants a sneak peek at your painting."

Mia nearly stumbled. "Uncle Rork? He wants to see my painting? Oh dear."

"Don't be nervous." Bea smiled. "Father adores your work."

"He does?" Mia asked, genuinely taken aback.

"Oh yes. He is forever praising it."

"That's the first I've heard of it."

Bea laughed. "Has your father ever given you a compliment directly?"

"No," Mia admitted. "Never."

"Well, there you have it. My father is the same. Mother had glowing things to say about my book, but Father only offered critiques."

"That sounds exactly like my father," Mia said.

Bea made a noise that sounded like a groan, "I think it's how men are."

"Or perhaps it's how fathers are," Mia mused. "Maybe they think being tough prepares us—so we won't fall apart when the real critics dig in."

Bea clapped her hands. "You might be right. Perhaps it's their strange way of protecting us."

"Ruff! Ruff!"

They turned in time to see Percy slide off a snowbank while Captyn—taking his big brother role seriously—nudged him upright with his nose before bounding away again.

"Speaking of being knocked down," Bea said with a grin.

AFTER PLAYTIME IN THE SNOW, THEY ALL TROMPED through the back entrance, the one used by family and servants—a practical little wing of the house that served as Baldwin Manor's unofficial mudroom. Snow-covered boots thudded up the steps, and the children burst through the door in a flurry of laughter and cold air.

The moment they crossed the threshold, the back hall erupted into cheerful chaos—mittens dropping, scarves loosening, coats half-sliding from small shoulders. Melted snow pooled on the stone tiles, quickly mopped up by the kitchen maids who were already waiting with towels.

Captyn and Percy barreled in after them, shaking off snowflakes like a pair of whirlwind blizzards. Percy wove between small legs, tail whipping joyfully, sending a hat flying and dragging a woolen scarf behind him like a victory ribbon. Eleanor squealed, and Josephine lunged after him. Betsy giggled and reached out to pat his damp, spotted head.

"Percy, behave!" Mia called, though amusement softened every syllable.

The Dalmatian paused, head tilted—pretending to consider obedience—then promptly bounded back toward the girls, who shrieked with delight.

Between giggles and good-natured scolding, Mia, Bea, Emma, and Ava ushered the girls through the mudroom and into the warm kitchen, helping them tug off their coats. Everything was hung neatly on the hooks near the hearth where the heat would dry them for the next snow-filled adventure.

After lunch, the entire family drifted toward the library—the true heart of Baldwin Manor at Christmastime. Flames crackled merrily in the fireplace, casting a golden light across the room, but it was the great Baldwin Christmas tree that commanded immediate attention. Nearly touching the ceiling beams, the towering fir was dressed in strands of cranberries, silver-tipped pinecones, delicate glass ornaments from Europe, gilded walnuts, and tiny candles in silver holders whose flames twinkled like captured starlight. The air held a faint hint of beeswax and wintergreen. Mia loved all the scents of Christmas almost as much as the bright, cheery colors.

Aunt Leila and Uncle Rork settled comfortably near the fire, while Liam and Margaret claimed the chairs beside them. Peter and Allie entered moments later from the nursery, each balancing one of the twins—Amy nestled against Allie's shoulder and Noah perched securely on Peter's hip, both blinking with wide, curious eyes at the spectacle of the tree.

Aunt Cornelia glided in with her usual flourish, smoothing her skirts as though she were about to take center stage. And, as tradition dictated, the household staff arrived too, aprons removed and hands freshly washed.

The Annual Baldwin Christmas Carol Sing-Along welcomed everyone—family and servants alike—and no one ever missed it.

Joseph, in his deep baritone, began leading them in carols, his voice rich enough to fill the room without effort. Clara settled at the piano, her fingers dancing across the keys as effortlessly as snowflakes on a winter breeze. The familiar strains of *God Rest Ye Merry, Gentlemen* rose and filled the library, a perfect harmony of family, laughter, and the glow of the Christmas season.

Mia slipped back into the warm bustle of the kitchen to refill an empty tray with gingerbread cookies when the door to the mudroom swung open, and a flurry of chilly air swept in.

"Any gingerbread and hot chocolate left for some weary travelers?" a familiar voice called.

"Johnny!" Mia squealed with delight as her foster brother strode in, stamping snow from his boots. She flew into his arms, and he swung her in a wide circle, laughing.

"Are we too late for the Annual Baldwin Christmas Carol Sing-Along," another voice said.

Mia turned and squealed again as she leaped into Adam's arms.

"Everyone will be thrilled that you two made it in time.

"Good. They won't be deprived of my legendary baritone," John declared, puffing up theatrically.

"I beg to differ," Adam countered reaching for a gingerbread man and biting its head off with gusto. "If a stellar performance is what you're looking for, I'm your man.

"I'm sure you're the best duo in the state."

"Well, technically we're a trio," Johnny said turning toward the door. "Look who we ran into on the way here."

A tall, broad-shouldered figure stepped into the kitchen, brushing snow from his black overcoat. The sight of him made Mia's heart leap so suddenly that she had to steady the plate of cookies.

Robert.

"I can't promise to match John's singing voice or Adam's showmanship," he said with a chuckle, "but I'll do my best."

"Right," John said, eyes twinkling. "I'll take that platter into the library before Adam inhales everything on it."

"Leave some for the children," she said.

"Maybe," Adam replied around a mouthful of gingerbread.

When she turned back to Robert, all the words she'd intended vanished.

"What's this?" he teased gently. "The ever-talkative Mia Baldwin is struck speechless? That's new."

"Oh, stop," she said, though her blush betrayed her. "It's just—you keep surprising me. Twice you've appeared out of nowhere."

He gave a soft laugh. "If we're counting properly, this is my third surprise appearance."

"Well—yes," she admitted, suddenly aware of how close he stood. "And I'm glad my parents invited you."

"They're wonderful people."

Mia beamed. "They are."

"And their daughter," he added, hazel eyes warming, "is equally remarkable."

Her stomach flipped. Oh, those eyes. Gold-flecked hazel, bright and glowing in the kitchen lamplight. "Careful, Dr. McDougall, if you keep flattering me, I might lose my heart."

He grew still. "And what would happen if you did?"

Her breath caught, and coherent thoughts drifted away. "I... I don't know," the gleam in his eyes captured her.

"Then perhaps," he leaned closer, "we should find out."

Before she could think, he drew her gently into his arms and kissed her.

She felt everything all at once—his coat still cold from outside, the faint scent of pine and winter air, the strength of his hand at her waist. Her heart raced so wildly she wondered if he felt it too. It was the most breathtaking moment of her life. Her first real kiss. Billy Anderson's stolen peck behind the schoolyard when she was twelve—didn't count anymore.

When they finally parted, Mia could scarcely breathe. "You... you kissed me."

"Yes." His lips curved. "I did."

"But there's no mistletoe above us."

"Ah..." He reached into his coat pocket. "I came prepared."

He lifted a small sprig of holly and ivy above her head.

Her breath fluttered. "Does that mean you're going to kiss me again?"

His voice dropped to a velvet murmur. "Do you want me to?"

Her answer was immediate, unguarded, and most emphatic. "Oh yes. I really do."

Robert chuckled—warm, delighted, confident—as he drew her close once more and kissed her again, giving her another memory, she knew she would carry for the rest of her life.

CHAPTER 6

A KISS BEFORE MIDNIGHT

Snow whispered against the windows of Baldwin Manor—the world outside wrapped in silver-blue stillness. Inside, the house had settled into the hushed quiet that followed a full day of celebration—children tucked into bed, parents whispering in their bedchambers as they wrapped a few final gifts for the stockings, candles snuffed in the halls one by one.

But in the library, one fire still burned low in the grate, its mellow amber glow flickering across shelves of leather-bound books and polished brass sconces.

Mia curled into Papa's old leather armchair—she was never able to sleep on Christmas Eve. As a child, she was far too excited. And tonight, her thoughts were wide awake, humming like a string plucked too tightly.

Percy lay sprawled before the fire, spotted belly to the heat, snoring softly. When Mia had slipped from her room earlier, he'd whimpered at the door, unwilling to be left behind.

"Very well," she'd whispered, stroking his silken ears. "But you must not wake the children."

He'd responded with a solemn "*woof*" and then had promptly fallen asleep in the library.

The wrapped gifts sat under the tree, ribbons shimmering faintly in the firelight. Among them lay her most precious one—the family portrait she'd painted for her parents, their thirtieth wedding anniversary approaching in June—thirty years—a lifetime. Mia could hardly imagine such a bond. Yet her parents still looked at one another like newlyweds. She had noticed earlier in the evening, during the Christmas carols, when Papa leaned toward Mama and whispered something that made her laugh like a girl again.

Mia's pencil moved lightly over the page of her sketchpad, lying open on her lap, shading in the curve of a vineyard trellis beneath a twilight sky. Sketching steadied her, shaped her thoughts, eased her restless heart. But the quiet ache remained.

She wanted what her parents had.

What Allie and Peter had.

What she saw echoed everywhere at Baldwin Manor—a home woven with deep, abiding love.

She exhaled a soft sigh.

A sudden shadow crossed the doorway.

She gasped and looked up, the pencil slipping from her fingers.

"Forgive me, I didn't realize anyone would be awake."

She knew that deep baritone instantly.

"Robert," she breathed, pressing a hand to her heart. "You startled me."

He stepped inside, closing the door gently behind him. He wore dark trousers and a half-open shirt, sleeves rolled up to the forearms, as though he'd abandoned sleep in frustration. His thick, wavy hair appeared as though he had been running his hands through it repeatedly.

"I couldn't sleep," he said, that rich voice reaching out to her in the quiet room. "I came down for a book."

"I couldn't sleep either," Mia replied, shifting upright. Percy thumped his tail once and greeted Robert, then flopped back onto the rug.

"I was sketching."

Robert stepped closer to the firelight, and her breath tangled. With the soft glow warming his skin, he looked almost unreal—as though he had just stepped out of a dream. Her dream.

"What are you working on?"

"Some ideas for your wine label."

His hazel eyes brightened. "May I see?"

She handed him the sketchbook, fingers brushing his. A tiny spark shot up her arm.

He lowered himself into the armchair beside hers, flipping through the pages slowly and methodically. Midway through, he paused, his gaze softening.

"These," he murmured, "are wonderful."

Heat flooded her cheeks.

"I thought perhaps a drawing of your home in the background," she said, "to show the winery as rooted in the land—and in you. A family business, not just a vineyard."

Oh heavens. Why had she said that? He was widowed. He had no children. She was assuming too much.

Robert looked up slowly. "Yes, that's exactly what I want."

Her pulse quickened.

He flipped to another sketch. "And this one is my favorite."

Mia swallowed. "Mine too."

"You'll have to come for another visit," he said, lifting his gaze to hers, "to sketch the house properly. If you're going to capture the spirit of my winery and estate, you'll need to spend time there."

Her breath caught. "Maybe a few more visits."

His voice lowered. "It might require many."

Heat blossomed beneath her skin.

"Of course," he added, though a teasing glint shone in his eyes, "your parents and sisters and brothers are welcome as well. Peter and Allie have already visited."

"They have? Allie never said a word."

"Perhaps it slipped her mind," he said, amusement curling his lips.

The grandfather clock in the corner began to toll.

"It's midnight."

Robert did not take his gaze from hers. "Merry Christmas, Mia."

Her heart fluttered. "Merry Christmas, Robert."

A daring, breathless impulse gripped her.

"Do you..." she ventured, "by any chance... have more mistletoe in your pocket?"

A low chuckle escaped him. "As a matter of fact..." He reached into his pocket and withdrew a small sprig of greenery. "I do."

"Then," she whispered, voice brushing the air like a feather, "I suppose we shouldn't let it go to waste."

"I completely agree." He rose from the chair and offered his hand. She took it, and he tugged her gently to her feet. When he bent toward her, the world seemed to tilt and fall away—leaving only the warmth of him, the tender certainty of his lips, and the slow, magical tide unfurling through her.

The fire crackled. Percy snored contentedly at their

feet. And everything—everything—seemed at once new and familiar, as though she had stumbled upon a wondrous truth she had always known, a discovery that embraced her and wrapped itself around her heart.

CHAPTER 7

A CHRISTMAS MORNING PROMISE

NORWALK, CONNECTICUT ~ CHRISTMAS DAY, 1888

*R*obert woke before dawn, staring up at the carved canopy above the guest bed, the faint winter light creeping through the frost-edged windows. He had rested, yes—but sleep had refused to come. His mind circled endlessly around a single image —Mia.

The stirrings inside him shifted, brightening in a way he thought impossible. Joy—even the fragile, exquisite joy of last night's stolen kisses—had a way of stirring old ghosts.

He shut his eyes, willing the past to stay quiet. But it didn't.

Years of hopelessness had gradually blackened everything.

Until Mia Baldwin.

Mia, who saw light where others saw shadows; color where others saw gray.

The promise of beginnings where others saw only endings.

But she was ten years younger. Bright, full of the kind of hope he feared he no longer deserved. Would she even want a man so marked by loss?

He didn't know. But the past few weeks made him dare to hope.

He reached for his coat hanging over the chair and withdrew the velvet pouch he had carried since her visit to the vineyard. He turned it over gently in his hand.

Not yet, he thought.

This morning belonged to Christmas—children's laughter, gifts, cinnamon, snow. But soon... the moment would come.

And he prayed that her answer would be what he hoped for.

THE BALDWIN LIBRARY GLOWED WITH WINTER SUNLIGHT, warm and golden as it caught the polished floors and flickered across the towering Christmas tree. The breakfast table—set up along the far wall—was a masterpiece in itself, with steaming platters of roasted potatoes, thinly sliced ham, juicy sausages, and crispy bacon, along with fluffy scrambled eggs topped with melted butter and cheese. There were pots of hot chocolate and coffee, bowls of sugared almonds, baskets of currant muffins and cinnamon bread, and a bowl of thick clotted cream, next to plates of preserved peaches and pears and a variety of jams and jellies.

Percy trotted happily underfoot, tail wagging dangerously near the platters.

"Percy, behave," Mia laughed just as Mrs. Bigelow swept in, carrying a silver tray heaped with warm muffins.

"Fresh from the oven," she announced as she set the platter down on the table.

On Emma's shoulder, Lord Wilby squawked loudly, "FRESH! FRESH!"

Percy barked. The twins squealed. Betsy clapped.

Chaos before breakfast.

Exactly as Christmas morning should be.

Mia approached Robert, who was standing by the window looking out over the snowy landscape. "You're in luck," she whispered, handing him a plate with a freshly baked muffin. "Everyone steals Mrs. Bigelow's muffins. So, I snuck one for you as soon as I could." Her heart did another somersault when his fingers brushed hers.

"You would have made a good thief," Robert said with a slow grin. The sunlight softened the hard lines of his face. He appeared... content. He seemed at home.

The children dashed about with baskets of presents. Liam was helping Eleanor and Josephine rearrange the furniture in their new dollhouse.

"Papa, we need a grandfather clock in the bathroom," Eleanor said.

"Whatever for?" her father replied, picking up the miniature.

"Because we need to time our bubble baths," Josephine added.

Liam turned to Margret with a question in his eyes.

"Papa, it's because Eleanor and Josephine always argue about who takes the longest in the bathroom," Betsy said with solemn wisdom as she leaned against her mother's shoulder. Everyone laughed as Margaret nodded in sage agreement.

Aunt Leila and Uncle Rork chuckled as they sipped their coffee.

Meanwhile, Peter balanced both Noah and Amy while Allie tried to feed her stalwart husband a bite of ham.

In the midst of the noise, Captyn—the enormous, spotted Great Dane—sat with an expression of serene anticipation, his tail thumping.

Mia narrowed her eyes. Captyn only looked that saintly when—

Sure enough, Adam leaned casually against the sideboard, covertly slipping a crisp strip of bacon into Captyn's waiting mouth as though engaged in the most natural business transaction in the world.

"Adam Baldwin!" Allie gasped, scandalized and amused all at once. "Are you feeding my dog bacon? He's already had his kibble."

Adam didn't even flinch. "What? He's a growing boy."

"He's six," Allie shot back.

"And the size of a steam carriage," Peter added. "If he gets any bigger, he'll have to sleep in the barn with the horses."

At this, Captyn gave a proud *woof*—as if the idea rather pleased him.

"Don't worry, Adam," John whispered. "I'll create a diversion next time."

"I heard that, Johnny," Allie warned.

Joseph Baldwin burst into a hearty laugh, the kind that shook his shoulders. Clara pressed a loving hand to his arm, smiling at the scene.

Even Aunt Cornelia, draped in ribbons and feathers, gave an uncharacteristically unguarded chuckle. "At this rate," she said, fluttering a handkerchief, "Captyn will require his own place setting at Christmas dinner."

Lord Wilby puffed his feathers and proudly shouted: "CAPTYN! CAPTYN!"

Emma froze. Ava groaned. "Lord Wilby, hush," they begged in perfect unison.

But the parrot was undeterred. He hopped onto the back of a chair, lifted one foot like he was conducting an orchestra, and hollered it again, "CAPTYN!"

This time, Captyn skidded across the rug, barking as if answering roll call.

Lord Wilby gave a satisfied nod.

Emma rubbed her temples. "Wonderful. Now he thinks he's the admiral of the house."

Lord Wilby squawked triumphantly, "CAPTYN!"

Captyn barked back.

Ava sighed. "We're living in a circus."

Joy and laughter filled every inch of Baldwin Manor.

Beatrice slipped to Mia's side and tugged her over to the hearth.

"I figured out my ending," she said in a low voice. "The heroine will propose to the hero, just as you suggested."

Mia's eyes widened. "Bea, that's wonderful!"

"It was your idea," Beatrice laughed. "Consider this my thank you."

Mia hugged her. "I'll be first in line to buy a copy."

A velvety baritone drew their attention, and they turned to regard Robert, who was laughing at something John had said, head tilted back, looking nothing like the somber man Mia had met two years ago.

Beatrice whispered, "Men like him are rare. If Aunt Cornelia brought a gentleman like that to my door, I'd allow him to recite dreadful sonnets all day."

Mia nearly spilled her tea. "Robert does not recite sonnets," she giggled. "But yes... he is rare."

Beatrice's smile softened. "He looks at you differently, you know."

"Bea—"

"And," her cousin continued, "on occasion, the heroine proposing isn't only a good ending for a book. It's also good advice in real life."

Mia blinked.

The room blurred a little—the tree, the fire, the gifts, the laughter—everything slid smoothly into place as if her heart had finally caught up with itself. "Bea," she whispered, "you're impossible."

"Maybe," Beatrice said, patting her arm. "And just maybe, I'm right."

Mia's pulse fluttered like a snowflake in a sudden draft.

"I think I'll take a stroll," she announced. "Walk off breakfast."

Beatrice's smile turned sly. "You do that, cousin."

Percy immediately leapt to his feet, tail swishing in eager approval.

Mia excused herself, heart beating far too quickly, and hurried toward the back staircase that led upstairs. In her chamber, she caught her breath long enough to pull out fresh parchment.

The words spilled faster than she could think, faster than she could question them.

A note.

Not long. Not elaborate. Just enough that he would understand...Mia hoped.

She folded it carefully and sealed it with a bit of wax, her hands trembling. Then she called to her maid.

"Helen, can you take this to Dr. McDougall. But not yet. Wait half an hour. Please."

Helen nodded, eyes sparkling with curiosity she politely did not voice.

"Deliver it exactly as instructed."

"Yes, miss."

Percy gave a single approving bark.

Mia straightened, exhaled deeply, and left her room, with her heart pounding in her ears. With Percy on her heels, she went down the back stairs to the mudroom where she'd left her cloak early that morning after returning from walking the pup.

Mia fastened her cloak, then paused. Something small and green hung from a hook beside the door. She tucked it into her pocket with a secret, smile.

"Well, Percy, here we go. Hopefully, the start of a new adventure."

The pup gave a small *woof* as Mia opened the back door and they stepped out into the bright, sunlit winter day.

Whatever happened next... she was finished hiding from her own heart. It was time to be brave. As Mia closed the door behind her, she felt the truth settle in her chest—warm, steady, impossible to set aside.

Today, she would follow that courage wherever it led.

CHAPTER 8

A ROMANTIC WONDERLAND

The Baldwin library—bookshelves heavy with stories of triumphs and trials, well-worn leather chairs drawn up to a roaring fireplace—soon grew altogether too warm.

The children shrieked over new toys, and Captyn snored loudly by the hearth. Robert wanted to ask Mia to go for a walk, but she had yet to return from whatever mysterious task she'd left to tend. And wherever she'd gone, Percy was likely with her.

"Dr. McDougall?"

He turned. Mia's maid, Helen, stood a few paces away, twisting her hands around a folded note.

"Yes?"

"This is for you, sir." She bobbed a little curtsy and offered the missive.

A familiar hand had written his name elegantly and neatly. His heart gave a sudden, irrational lurch.

"Thank you," Robert said.

Helen retreated toward the door—her curiosity unmistakable even from halfway across the room.

He stepped into a quiet corner and opened the note.

Dear Robert,

If you have had your share of muffins and would enjoy a brief respite from the loud and raucous chorus of Christmas morning with the Baldwins, may I suggest a walk in this winter wonderland?

Percy and I will be in the garden gazebo at noon.

Mia

No flourish. No explanation.

He checked his pocket watch. It was five minutes to noon. His pulse quickened.

She wanted to see him. Alone. Away from the warmth and noise and safety of the house.

He folded the note and slipped it into his pocket next to the small velvet pouch.

And with a smile, he anticipated Mia's surprise when her suggestion for a walk turned into something she was not expecting, but hopefully would welcome.

The path to the garden gazebo was lightly powdered with snow. The air was sharp and clean, the kind of crisp cold that made each deep breath awaken your senses.

From a distance, Baldwin Manor carried the charm of a storybook world—windows glowing with soft light, smoke curling from chimneys, wreaths dark against the pale stone. The gazebo stood at the far edge of the garden, its white columns and railings frosted, its roof edged in icicles shimmering in the winter light.

Mia was already there.

She sat on the built-in bench along the inner railing, cloak wrapped around her, a dusting of snow on the hem as if it had tried to claim her and failed. Percy, by her side, tail wagging when he saw Robert. He didn't bark—just gave a low, delighted rumble, as though he, too, understood this moment was different.

Mia stood as Robert approached, pushing back her hood. The sunlight caught the blue of her eyes, making them sparkle.

"Robert," she said, breath clouding the air. "You came."

"As if I'd ignore a summons from Miss Mia Baldwin," he replied, trying for humor. His voice sounded gruffer than he'd intended. "You'll ruin me for ordinary invitations."

A small smile tugged at her mouth, but she seemed... nervous. He could see it in the way her gloved fingers twisted together, in the way she kept glancing down at Percy, as if drawing courage from that tilted head and wagging tail.

"I wanted to speak with you."

He stepped into the gazebo, wood creaking beneath his boots. The cold brushed his face, and yet the air between them seemed to crackle like sparks from a fire.

"I'm glad you do," he said. "Because I very much wanted to speak with you as well."

Her cheeks flushed a lovely pink that had nothing to do with the temperature.

"Ah, Well. That's... good."

Percy gave an encouraging *"woof,"* settling in for a performance.

For a moment, neither of them spoke.

Then Mia drew a breath—the kind of breath someone takes before jumping into deep water.

"Robert, I have been giving this a great deal of thought. And, well, even if it was my idea to begin with, I had intended it to be for Beatrice's story. And when she told me she decided to have the heroine be brave enough to speak first, I was pleased, but then she said that it might even work in real life, and at first, I didn't know what she meant, and then of course I figured it out and...well, Beatrice can be rather cheeky. Still, she had a point, so I decided to try it. Be the heroine and speak first, and I thought—"

She faltered, eyes widening. "Oh dear, that sounded so much better in my head."

He grinned. "If it helps, I think you are brave enough to do anything you want."

"Truly?"

"Yes, truly."

"I was trying to be," she admitted. "Trying to be brave, that is. Because... because I don't want to look back on my life and wonder why I never said what was in my heart."

Her words landed like stones in a still pond, sending ripples through him.

Robert's throat tightened. Every instinct told him to spare her, to step in, to rescue her from having to say something difficult. But another part of him—the part that had watched her face light up under the Christmas tree, that rejoiced when she kissed him back without hesitation—knew she deserved her moment. Her say.

So, he stood and waited. "Mia, go on, please."

She pressed her lips together, then lifted her chin, meeting his eyes.

"Robert McDougall," she said, voice trembling but clear, "I am very much in love with you. And I would like to know if you would consider marrying me."

The words had come out in a rush, tumbling over each other, ending in a whispered "me."

He stared at her.

She stared back, color flooding her cheeks, eyes

wide as if just realizing she'd leapt without checking for ground.

Percy lifted his head, waiting for a verdict.

And then, to his own surprise, Robert laughed. A short, astonished, utterly delighted laugh that burst from deep in his chest.

Mia recoiled slightly. "Oh no, that's—oh, I knew this was a terrible idea," she whispered, beginning to turn away. "Please forget—"

"Mia," he said, stepping closer. He caught her hands in his before she could flee. "Mia. You have not said anything foolish. You have only beaten me to it."

She blinked. "I... what?"

He smiled, still a little stunned. "I had the same idea. I have been pacing like a madman for weeks trying to decide when and how to ask you the very same question."

"You... you were going to propose?"

"Yes." His voice steadied. "I *am* going to propose."

She swayed slightly where she stood. "Oh."

"And you," he added, "are brave. Braver than you know. I have known grown men with less courage than you've shown today."

Her eyes shone with unshed tears and doubt. "Robert, you don't have to—"

"Yes," he interrupted. "I do. There are words I need to speak—words I should have said some time ago." He drew a breath, feeling the cold air fill his lungs, feeling the weight of years settle and then finally began to ease. "You remember I told you my wife, Adele, died in child-birth," he said.

Mia's fingers tightened in his. "You don't owe me—"

"I owe us honesty. If I ask you to share my life, you deserve to know what came before."

She swallowed, then nodded.

"Adele and I married young," he began. "Far too young, some would say. I was a medical student, full of theories and ambition, and she was bright. Laughing. Kind. We wanted a family immediately, but it took years before she conceived. When she finally did, I thought that God, or fate, or the universe had decided to be merciful."

His jaw tightened. "The birth went badly. Too fast in some ways, too slow in others. Complications, I did not yet know how to manage. I did everything I could. She died despite all I knew. Our baby died. And I—" His voice caught. "I was a doctor who could not save his own family. I carried that failure in my bones for years."

Mia's eyes filled. "You were not a failure."

"I believed I was, and for a long time. Peter pulled me through those first months. He practically dragged me into the coroner's office, said if I was going to live in the dark, I might as well make it useful. So, I did. And it kept me moving. But it also kept me in those shadows."

He met her gaze.

"And then I met you."

Her lips parted slightly.

"You walked into my house, with your quick questions and your brilliant eyes and your paintings that saw more than most people ever do. You reminded me that the world wasn't only full of endings. It had color. Texture. Emotion. You made me want to create life again instead of cataloguing the dead."

"The vineyard."

"Yes, the vines. The land. A place meant to grow and endure. A family business, passed down from one generation to the next. Roots that would outlast me, outlast the grief, outlast the darkness. But there is only one woman I wish to build that life with."

He released one of her hands long enough to reach into his coat. The velvet pouch felt heavier than it had that morning. Or perhaps he understood its weight differently now. "Mia Baldwin," he said, sinking to one knee in the snow.

She gasped, one hand flying to her mouth.

Percy sniffed Robert's hair as if to confirm this was indeed happening, then sat with grave solemnity.

Robert opened the pouch and revealed a simple but lovely ring—gold, with a modest cluster of small diamonds that caught the sparkling winter light.

"I love you," he said. "For your kindness. Your

courage. Your fierce sense of what is right. For the way you see the world in color when others see only gray. I loved you long before I admitted it to myself. Will you marry me, Mia? Will you build this new life, this family, this future with me?"

Tears spilled freely down her cheeks now, bright against the flush of cold.

"Oh, Robert," she whispered, voice breaking. "Your proposal is so much better than mine."

He laughed, joy bursting through him like a sudden thaw.

"Thank you," he said. "But does that mean... you're saying yes?"

She didn't answer with words at first.

She launched herself at him, nearly knocking him backward into the snow. He caught her, arms closing around her waist, laughter mingling with hers as Percy erupted into joyous barking.

"Yes," she said finally, breathless, her forehead resting against his. "Yes, yes, yes—I'm saying yes."

Percy threw back his head and let out a long, delighted howl that echoed off the snow and stone. In the distance, a startled crow complained and flew off.

Robert, still holding her, spun her once in a circle, her cloak flaring, snowflakes catching in her hair. She laughed—a pure, bright sound he wanted to hear every day for the rest of his life.

When he finally set her down, she stayed close, hands on his chest, eyes shining.

"Oh," she said suddenly, a secretive glint appearing. "I nearly forgot."

"Forgot what?" he asked, still dizzy with happiness.

She reached into her cloak pocket and drew out a small sprig of green leaves and berries gleaming against the white of her glove.

"Mistletoe," she said. "I thought we might need it."

"You came prepared," he murmured, amused.

"Of course," she replied. "If we're making promises for a lifetime, we might as well seal them properly."

She handed him the mistletoe, and he lifted it above their heads with one hand.

Robert looked up at the tiny bit of green, then back at the petite, incredible, beautiful woman who had somehow led him from death into life.

"Yes," he said. "Let's."

And as Percy circled them in delighted, barking loops while snow fell in soft, quiet flakes around the gazebo, Robert kissed his future wife, this time under mistletoe, and with all the certainty in the world.

CHAPTER 9

A SPRING WEDDING AT BALDWIN MANOR

NORWALK, CONNECTICUT, MAY 11, 1889

$\mathcal{M}$ay had arrived in a riot of color and scent. The manor gardens—visible through the tall chapel windows—were a mix of tulips, daffodils, peonies, and early roses, their petals trembling in the warm spring breeze. Sunlight poured through the glass, gilding everything it touched—the polished pews, the stone pillars, even the faint motes of dust floating lazily in the air.

Inside, the Baldwin family chapel shimmered with new life.

Mia stood in the vestibule near the arched windows, her white silk gown luminous in the morning light. The delicate lace at her shoulders framed her collarbones like frostwork, though nothing about her felt cold. Warmth hummed through her—excitement, anticipation, and a breathless joy that threatened to lift her off the floor.

Clara, wearing a powder blue gown with pearly lace, fluttered behind her, fussing with the silver and blue ribbons woven into Mia's hair. Smoothing curls with the urgency of a woman preparing her daughter for both matrimony and battle.

"Too tight—no, too loose—oh, heavens," Clara murmured, simultaneously wiping at her eyes and wrestling with a stray strand of Mia's hair.

Mia's maid, Helen, who had been hovering discreetly nearby, stepped forward with a calm smile. "Allow me, Mrs. Baldwin," she said gently, taking over the task with practiced hands.

"Mama," Mia said softly, touching her mother's cheek, "I'm not going to fall apart."

"You'd better not," Clara sniffed, "because I just might."

Emma and Ava—her bridesmaids—twirled in their matching silvery-blue gowns, the pale silk catching the light like raindrops sliding down a windowpane.

"You look beautiful, Mia," Emma declared.

"Perfect," Ava agreed, with a firm nod. "Utterly perfect."

"And you two look like springtime personified," Mia said, gathering them both into a quick hug.

Allie, walking in with Captyn at her side, beamed at her mother and sisters. "Are we ready?" She moved with the grace of someone long accustomed to balancing elegance with impending motherhood. Her indigo silk gown made a striking contrast to her red hair, and Captyn—sporting a matching bow tied around his muscular neck—heeled beside her with surprising decorum, as though he fully understood the seriousness of the occasion.

"You look radiant, darling," Allie said, kissing Mia's cheek. "Now don't cry yet, because if you do, then I'll start, and then my face will turn splotchy, and you know how dreadful I'll look—red hair and splotchy skin is not a winning combination."

Clara dabbed at her eyes again. "Good heavens, those hair ribbons will be the death of me. Helen, do they look fine to you?"

"They look perfect, Mrs. Baldwin," Helen said with a reassuring smile. "Miss Mia, you are a sight."

"They don't look too tight? Or too loose?" Clara pressed.

"No," everyone replied in unison.

Percy barked in agreement, tail whipping the air like a metronome attempting its own fugue.

Lord Wilby swooped down from his perch, landing on the back of a chair. "TOO TIGHT! TOO LOOSE!"

Emma burst out laughing. "Wilby, you dreadful creature!"

A knock at the door signaled the time had come. "Joseph Baldwin, father of the bride, reporting for duty," her father called from the hallway.

Clara gave a soft chuckle. "Darling daughter, I shall leave you now. I cannot wait to see you walk down the aisle with your father." She kissed Mia's cheek, gave her hands one last, steadying squeeze, and slipped out with Allie, Captyn, and Helen following close behind.

The string quartet began to play. The chapel hushed. Mia inhaled deeply.

Emma and Ava made their way down the aisle, Lord Wilby perched proudly on Emma's arm like an avian dignitary. Percy trotted beside Ava, a smart blue-and-silver bow fastened at his neck—the perfect match to the wedding colors, and worn with all the gravity of a seasoned groomsman.

Her father bent his head toward hers. "Ready, my girl?"

And she was.

Then Mia stepped into the chapel on her father's arm, sunlight gathering around her like a quiet benediction. The guests rose, a wave of color and warmth lifting to meet her, ushering her forward.

Robert cut a striking figure in his tailored navy suit, the silver tie catching just enough light to lend him an air of quiet nobility. He had neatly combed his hair, save for one wayward lock that had rebelliously escaped—Mia's favorite kind.

But it was his eyes—those golden-hazel depths—that truly stole her breath.

Tender. Awed. Overflowing with love.

"You're late," he murmured when she reached him, his smile sweeping through her like sunlight on deep water.

"Two dogs and a parrot delayed me," she said, her voice trembling with joy.

Laughter rippled through the chapel.

Robert took her hands, steady and warm, grounding her as the minister began. The world softened around them—the scent of roses, the shimmer of stained glass, the flicker of candles.

And then it was time.

Robert inhaled, and when he spoke, his voice was steady, rich, full of feeling she felt down to her bones.

"Through storm and calm," he began, "through every day we're given, I will choose you, Mia, again and again. I will love you fiercely and stand beside you in all joys and all sorrows, in every quiet and extraordinary moment we share."

Mia's eyes blurred, her heart swelling with so much love she felt like she was floating.

She whispered her vows in return. "And I, you. Through laughter, through sunshine, through every ordinary and extraordinary moment, I'll never lose sight of home—because home is you."

Robert pressed his forehead to Mia's briefly before they sealed their vows with a tender, perfect kiss.

The bells began to ring. The guests cheered. And in the warm light of May, surrounded by laughter and love, Robert and Mia stepped into the first moments of their forever.

EPILOGUE

A HARVEST OF BLESSINGS

FAIRFIELD CONNECTICUT ~ THANKSGIVING, 1890

*T*wilight brushed the hills of Fairfield in strokes of lavender and blue as Robert and Mia stepped into the quiet warmth of the tasting room, where the firelight glowed against polished oak barrels. The air smelled of oak staves, spice, and fermenting fruit, a comforting blend that had come to feel like the heartbeat of their new life.

Robert lifted a small bottle from the counter. "Just a taste," he said, uncorking it carefully. "The port has rested long enough to give us a preview."

Mia's eyes sparkled. "A private tasting... How wonderfully daring of you, Dr. McDougall."

He poured them each a sip—ruby, warm, velvety. Their glasses caught the firelight like two tiny lanterns in the dim room.

"To discoveries," he said.

Their glasses touched.

The sound was soft, intimate.

They tasted. The port glowed warmly down their throats, rich with spice and hope.

Mia exhaled, a soft, pleased sigh. "Oh, Robert... this is wonderful."

Her voice—soft, warm, full of pride—hit him harder than the wine.

Before he could second-guess himself, he leaned in.

She met him halfway.

Their kiss was slow, lingering...as warm as the wine they'd just sipped. A kiss made for twilight, for gratitude, for the life they were building.

When they parted, breath misting between them, she whispered, "If we stay here any longer, the family will believe we've run off."

He laughed. "Then we best make our escape."

She tucked her hand into the crook of his arm, and together they stepped out into the crisp late-afternoon air.

The first whispers of winter hushed the world

outside. The vines—wrapped in burlap and straw—stood quiet and proud, catching pale gleams of fading light as the couple crossed the path to the waiting carriage.

Robert helped her in, climbed in beside her, and flicked the reins.

The short ride back to the manor was peaceful: the crunch of wheels on frosted earth, the rhythmic sway of the carriage, Mia pressed close beneath her cloak, their hands intertwined beneath the blanket.

Ahead, the manor glowed like a beacon against the deepening dusk—warm windows, rising laughter, and the smell of Thanksgiving supper drifting faintly into the cold evening air.

When they stepped through the door, the warmth embraced them. The aroma of roast turkey, sage stuffing, and fresh rolls filled the air—familiar voices wrapped around them like a welcome.

Clara and Joseph sat near the hearth, each holding a twin—Lily nestled against Clara's shoulder, Leo perched sturdily on Joseph's knee. The moment the twins spotted their parents, both babies burst into delighted squeals.

Mia kissed the soft downy heads of her babies, then, taking Lily from Clara's lap, she smoothed her daughter's dark curls. The little girl gave a delighted coo and a fierce tug on her mother's necklace.

Robert leaned in and kissed Lily's cheek before turning to Leo. He scooped the boy into his arms, laughing as Leo kicked with such enthusiasm that he nearly catapulted himself out of Robert's arms. "There now, steady, my lad."

Leo gurgled, grabbed a handful of his father's dark green tie, and pulled with purpose.

Robert kissed the boy's warm forehead, inhaling that comforting baby scent that still stunned him with its sweetness.

Mia stepped in close beside him, Lily nestled against her shoulder, Leo wriggling proudly against his, the four of them wrapped in warmth and firelight.

It struck him with such force, such quiet awe, that his breath caught.

This was everything.

How did I ever live without this?

Without her.

Without them.

Inside the dining room, the long polished table gleamed beneath an elegant centerpiece of chrysanthemums, dahlias, hydrangeas, and trailing grapevines, with tiny pumpkins hollowed to cradle flickering candles. Their warm glow shimmered across silver, crystal, and polished wood, turning the table into a cozy harvest tableau.

Allie held baby Amanda on her hip; the infant promptly attempted to eat Allie's necklace.

Percy thumped his tail by the hearth; Captyn rested at his side, like a tolerant older brother.

Above them, Lord Wilby perched on the back of a chair.

Meanwhile, Noah and Amy—Allie and Peter's exuberant twins—toddled beneath the table, clutching rolls like stolen treasure.

"All right, you two bandits," Peter warned, "hand those over, or no turkey for you."

"NO TURKEY FOR ME!" Lord Wilby squawked.

"Hush," Emma and Ava said in perfect unison.

Laughter rippled through the room.

Then Aunt Cornelia swooped in wearing rust-colored silk and a determined sparkle.

"Adam, darling," she cried, beelining toward the unfortunate gentleman, "I met the loveliest young woman in the city—a flautist of exceptional talent—"

The entire Baldwin clan groaned.

"A flautist?" Adam repeated miserably.

"She plays the flute exquisitely," Cornelia insisted. "What if I invite her for Christmas?"

"Oh, good Lord," Adam muttered. "Someone hide me until the spring thaw."

John leaned over and stage-whispered to Adam, "Count your blessings, she didn't say tuba."

Robert chuckled as the Baldwin chaos swirled around him. This noise, this family, this warmth—it filled corners of his heart he once believed permanently empty.

A figure entered the dining room with a polite bow —Barnes the Second, nephew of the original Baldwin Manor butler, trained impeccably but considerably more relaxed than his famed uncle.

"Dr. and Mrs. McDougall," he said warmly, "your Thanksgiving supper is ready to be served."

Robert tightened his hold on Leo and stepped forward.

"This is our first Thanksgiving here," he began, voice thick with emotion. "And the first in my life where this house—and this land—truly feels like home."

Mia's eyes met his. Glowing. Loving.

"For many years, I did not believe such a thing was possible," he continued. "But Mia changed that. She changed everything."

Lily cooed against her mother's shoulder. Leo curled his tiny hand around Robert's thumb.

Robert lifted his glass of pale-gold sparkling wine— the very first vintage from the vines he had tended with hope he scarcely dared to name.

"To my wife, whose love brought light back into my life. To my children, who show me every day how blessed the future can be. And to all of you—our family

—my family." He raised his glass. "To family, hearth and home."

Glasses lifted. "To family, hearth and home!" everyone echoed.

Wilby shrieked, "HOME! HOME!"

Robert leaned down and kissed Mia as applause broke out.

Percy barked.

Captyn huffed.

And Leo—excited by the cheers—stuffed Robert's silver tie directly into his mouth.

"I suppose that's his toast," Robert said, laughing.

"He approves," Mia murmured, snuggling Lily closer. "And so do I."

Outside, delicate snowflakes drifted over the sleeping vines.

Inside, Robert carved the turkey and counted his blessings.

I hope you enjoyed *A Match for Mischief*, Book 3 in my American Heiresses Series

If you have a moment, I would be truly grateful if you could leave a review—or even just a quick rating—on Amazon or Goodreads.

Reviews are more than kind words to an author... they help other readers discover the book, keep the series going strong, and they absolutely make my day.

(Truly. At 90, I consider every good review an extra candle on the cake!)

Thank you for spending time with my characters and for being part of my reading family. Your support means the world.

Please scan or click on the following QR code below to leave a review.

Warmly,

Gail

STORIES, SHENANIGANS & THE OCCASIONAL COOKIE RECIPE

Dear Reader,

If you'd enjoy a little extra joy in your inbox, please consider signing up for my newsletter by scanning or clicking on the following QR code.

No spam—ever. Just a friendly monthly note from me filled with cheerful updates, book news, giveaways, funny stories, and the occasional recipe... usually inspired by whatever mischief I've gotten into.

Hope to see you there!

Warmly,

Gail

FREE PREVIEW 1

THE MEMORABLE MRS. DEMPSEY

*L*eila Dempsey stepped onto the sun-dappled veranda and froze. She stared at her husband and pressed a trembling hand to her heart that all but ceased to beat.

Hank Dempsey leaned against the wall, close to a riot of red curls. His lips hovered over a lush, pouty mouth. The young woman threw back her mane and laughed, a deep throaty sound—the laughter of a woman who knew what she wanted and went after it. Sissy Lanweihr wanted Hank.

The chatter stopped, and all eyes turned to Leila, not five feet away from her mother, Priscilla, and her society friends.

Not again—blather for the ladies' morning teatime.

Her eyes skittered to her mother, who threw her a warning glance. The matriarch had not a wisp of gray hair out of place, not a wrinkle in her high-collared lavender gown. Her smooth face was stoic, and icy blue eyes censured Leila.

Everything in Leila screamed rebellion.

Hank turned his head toward his wife. His bloodshot eyes fell on her, and his lips tilted up into a sardonic smile.

Another piece of Leila's soul shattered. She fought humiliation and stared at the faces that swam before her blurred vision. Leila sailed down the broad steps with all the dignity she could muster. She turned and paused. The Catskill Mountain House stood proudly perched on a ledge surrounded by imposing mountain peaks. Once a cheerful place, nothing made her cheery these days. She drew a shuddering breath and immersed herself in the view of rolling forests below. A brook meandered through the lush vegetation, sparkling in the sunlight.

A sob escaped her. Hank's betrayal tore at her like talons. She lifted her voluminous skirts and ran down the slope toward the water. A breeze sighed through the long grass and set seed heads swaying in its wake.

Away from prying eyes, she stopped. Harsh breaths escaped her constricted chest, and tears fell. She clenched her hands, trying to combat the pain of infidelity. Her stomach churned, and bile crawled up her throat.

"He's killing my love." The breeze swallowed her whisper. Her dream marriage to a dashing author had become a nightmare. Sissy, with her brazen red hair and even bolder behavior, sabotaged our marriage. She's wanted Hank since meeting him at our betrothal. Leila would never forget the look of malice and anger on Sissy's face at her wedding.

Her knees buckled, and she sank onto the grass. Tears dripped from her lashes. Watery stains spread in uneven circles on her soft-white day dress. Leila sniffed and dashed the tears away with her fists.

"I hate her—hate that Sissy Lanweihr with her fiery red hair and...and worldly ways."

Leila ripped off her fashionable bonnet and yanked the pins from her coiffured brunette hair, sending it tumbling over her shoulders to her waist. Sweat trickled down Leila's bosom. The corset suffocated her, like her marriage.

"I want to be free." She blinked and stared at a pearl-topped pin in her hand. "Do I want to be free?" She swallowed hard. "Do I still love him?" A mirthless laugh burst from her lips. "Hank has never said he loves me—maybe he doesn't. Maybe he never did."

"Leila! Leila!"

Her head snapped around. "Mama," she whispered and scrambled in the long grass, hunting for hairpins. She fumbled with her mass of hair, trying to restore the coiffure.

"Leila, where are you? Don't make me come down there to fetch you."

Leila's mouth tightened, and her fingers clenched around five pins. One pricked her, and she gasped. She dropped the hairpins and stared at a drop of blood oozing from her thumb and wiped it off with a blade of grass.

"I will not go back," she muttered. She crawled behind a tree and leaned against the massive trunk, facing the brook.

"This is most inappropriate, Leila. I shall deal with you later," her mother shouted.

A giggle bubbled up, and she put a hand over her mouth. *I won.* The high collar of the dress stifled her. She peeked around the tree to see if her mother had left and released the pearl buttons. A breathy sigh escaped her as the breeze brushed her skin exposed above the chemise. Leila looked down at the bodice.

Leila and her two best friends, Clara and Olivia, agreed they'd no longer wear the horrible corsets. However, while Clara and Olivia had rid themselves of their corsets, Leila's mother forbid her to honor her part of the agreement. They'd argued about it often, but Leila lost, and the corset remained. An uneven battle, conformity always won.

Leila flopped back and lay spread-eagle, looking up at the leaves dancing in the light breeze overhead. *Has my life ever been free?* The warmth of the sun tickled her skin like a feather. She wanted to rip off her clothes, feel the sun caress her bare skin. Oh, to be free of restraints. Free of rules. Free of a philandering husband.

She closed her eyes, breathed in the fresh mountain air, and giggled again. She'd already overstepped the bounds of propriety.

Her conduct would scandalize her mother and the genteel ladies at the Mountain House.

Water gurgled around rocks. Crickets chirped, and birds flitted through the dappled shade. Nature's orchestra soothed her troubled spirit, reminding her of carefree summers when she played games on the brook's mossy rocks. She'd challenged each rock to stand steady, hopping over them until she reached the other side. Oh, to do that anew.

Why not? She jumped to her feet and surveyed the swollen brook. Water rushed over rocks in foaming eddies, leaving a few exposed as it raced to a dark green pool. *I can do this.*

She stepped onto a moss-covered rock inches from the edge of the brook. Water swirled around her skirt like champagne, soaking her hem. With each step, her exhilaration rose. *I wish Hank were with me.* She frowned. *No, I don't!* The smooth, black stone sparkled, peeking above the water like an iridescent jewel between the mosses, beckoning her.

She set her foot down and stepped onto the rock, held her breath, and jumped to the next one. Once stable, she put her weight on another. Buoyed by success, she planted herself. It held. Once more a child, she laughed, unburdened by the constraints of society. She held her arms out like the spars of a topsail. Halfway across the brook, confidence replaced caution. She skipped across three rocks, whooped with joy—six left to go.

Her tongue poked from the corner of her mouth as she balanced. The rock wobbled. Her foot slipped on slimy moss. She gasped, searching for a secure foothold. Arms flailing, she fought to regain her balance. Too late.

She squeezed her eyes shut and hit the rocks with a bruising impact. Icy water engulfed her, stealing her breath. She floundered and clutched at the slippery rocks, but her sodden garments hampered her efforts, and the strong current carried her away. The brook, now the enemy, tumbled her faster toward the pool. A scream tore from her throat before her head slammed into a rock.

ROCK MILBURN SMILED AS HE SURVEYED THE VIEW OF THE early morning dew glistening in the sun. Art had been a lifelong pursuit for Rork Millburn. He hoped to paint several small works during his stay at the Mountain House. His easel sat on a flat, grassy area above a brook. The aroma of the juicy oil paints culled fond memories of the times he'd spent in the Alps. He stepped back to examine his work. Satisfied he'd captured the early sun-drenched mountains lush with wispy grasses, pine trees, and fields of flowers, he was almost finished. Just a few more touches.

Movement drew his attention. A woman crossing the brook caught his artist's eye. He took in the image of her day dress flying up as she leaped from one rock to the next like a water sprite. Something stirred in him, something not related to the warm sun, earthy forest smells, or imposing mountains. His keen eyes picked out her exquisite features. The sun danced on her hair that fell in lustrous waves to a slender waist. He set down his palette and scrambled among paints and brushes until he found his monocle. He screwed it to his eye and snatched a breath at her beauty and those luscious lips, a mouth made for kisses. A kiss he could only imagine. He mentally shook free his fanciful imaginings. *Fool, just paint!*

A scream echoed across the valley and shot through him like a bullet. He scanned the brook below. "What in the world?" His breath caught in his throat.

The woman had vanished. Her bonnet still lay on the grass.

"My God!" Rork raced down the hill, the wind whipping his hair. Lungs burning, he slid down a steep drop to the brook. He searched the river, running along the bank where he last saw the woman. "Damn, where are you?" He wiped the sweat from his brow.

A tangle of dark hair floated to the surface, then sank again.

Rork ripped off his jacket and shoes and plunged into the frigid water. His heart pumped faster with each stroke as he swam to where he'd seen her hair. *Please God, let me get to her in time.* He glimpsed whitish fabric and dived. *There she is.* He grabbed her arm and kicked hard, surging to the surface. Currents had carried them to rocks farther downstream, and the weight of her soaked dress impeded progress. He fought the river's pull and dragged the woman from the water, lifting her into his arms.

She moaned, stirred, and convulsed, vomiting water.

Thank God she's alive. The uneven terrain caused him to slip and stumble.

His legs ached as he knelt, still holding her limp body in his arms. Thick, black lashes contrasted with her ivory skin. The soaked dress clung to her, outlining her petite figure, making her seem helpless—fragile. The disarray of her skirt and petticoats exposed her long legs to above her knees. He shuddered.

Her head rolled to one side, she groaned, and a slender hand fluttered to her throat.

He stared at the enlarging bloodstain on his shirtsleeve. *She's injured.* He set her down with care on the grass and bent to examine the back of her head. Thick blood seeped into her hair. He parted her tresses and exposed a gash. Ripping off his shirtsleeve, he pressed it to the wound, staunching the blood. She flinched and tried to twist away. He withdrew his hand. "Can you hear me?"

Her lips moved, but her only answer was a silent puff of air.

A rosy tint crept into her pale cheeks. A stab in his chest, sharp and sweet, moved through him, as though he'd witnessed da Vinci's *Mona Lisa* come alive. Icy dread cooled his thoughts of romance.

He didn't know what to do. He figured she had to be

a guest at the Catskill Mountain House as there were no other habitations in the area.

"Please, wake up. You're safe now."

No response.

Hands trembling from both the cold and the emotion she invoked in him, he returned her skirt to its proper position and attempted to button her bodice. Her chest rose and fell with each breath, distracting him. His huge hands fumbled with the small pearl buttons.

"Damn ham-hands," he said. "How does anyone ever get these buttons fastened?" He struggled on. "Damn." He slipped his hand inside her bodice to get a better grip, and his fingers brushed against the soft skin of her bosom.

The woman stirred.

He withdrew his hand, wiped the water from her eyes, and smoothed the hair from her face. "Hush. It's all right. You'll be fine."

She pushed at his clumsy fingers. Her thick lashes lifted, unveiling dark blue eyes.

"Lord above, your eyes are deep sapphire." The ground beneath Rork swayed as he tumbled into the depths of her lucent gaze.

I HOPE YOU ENJOYED THIS **FREE PREVIEW** OF *THE Memorable Mrs. Dempsey*, Book 1 in The American Heiresses Series. Each novel in the series is a stand-alone story and can be read in any order—though they're especially delightful when enjoyed in sequence.

If you'd like to keep reading *for free* with Kindle Unlimited, simply click or scan the QR code below.

FREE PREVIEW 2

THE UNFORGETTABLE MISS BALDWIN

NEW YORK CITY ~ NOVEMBER 1, 1886

Joseph Baldwin slammed his hand on the desk and waved a stack of complaint letters in his daughter's face. "These are evidence of our readers' objections to your presence at a dance hall and your support for women's suffrage."

Allie Baldwin wiped her sweaty hands on her dress, her stomach dropping with nauseating abruptness. "This is impossible, Papa, to stand here and listen to your tirade."

"You are dabbling in dangerous waters. There's no place for women in politics. They will never earn the right to vote," he said, pointing to Allie with his inking pen.

Allie clamped her hand to her throat and waited for a moment, gathering her thoughts. "Papa, not that long ago, the authorities arrested women in Rochester, New York, after they illegally tried to vote in the presidential election. I am sure they will try to vote again. These women will starve and sacrifice their lives for their rights."

"I'm aware, but they disobeyed the law. Jailing them is just punishment."

Allie gasped and slammed her hand against her mouth, then lowered it as she spoke. "It's shameful. The women did not deserve jail."

"No daughter of mine would ever be so bold. Your disagreement shows me you do not understand the seriousness of these issues."

"I'm sorry, Papa, but you are wrong. There's a law stating that single women can vote if they own property. That's ridiculous since the law stops them from owning property. It's demoralizing. How dare men think women cannot handle voting. We must change the law. At the moment, my concern is today's rally and why you forbid me to go."

"Stop this stubbornness. The fight is going nowhere, and it's dangerous."

Allie's face felt flushed. "This is my opportunity to

write about women's rights, voting, and freedom. Assign another reporter to society issues, please, Papa."

The banjo clock's *tick, tick, tick* evoked memories of Mama's lessons to mind her manners. The steady rhythm usually calmed Allie. But not today. A daughter should not defy her father, much less her superior.

"Papa, remember your promise?"

He stroked the edge of his thick mustache. "My promise?"

She gripped the edge of his desk. "Yes, you promised after graduation, my writing could include public issues like this suffrage rally."

"Maybe you had better talk to your mother."

"Why? Does Mama disapprove?"

"Our concern is your safety."

"What? That's absurd." She grabbed the side chair by the window, rolled it to his desk, and sat, her spine straight as Mama's knitting needle. She smoothed the peacock-blue, high-collared dress billowing over her knees and stared into her father's face. "I do not see what could be harmful. I am wearing my tattered coat and hat. No one will bother with an old lady in rags."

"Once again, you're putting yourself in . . ." Allie's father hesitated and cleared his throat. "This is an unsubstantial argument. You cannot create subterfuge with a coat and hat." He pointed to the stack of letters.

"These letters are not jesting. Serious readers wrote disparaging remarks about you."

She clasped her hands to her chest. "About me?"

"I'm afraid so. Our readers question your visit to a dance hall. It might well have been a brothel."

"Brothel? It was not. I saved a young girl from being accosted. What are the objections?"

His forehead furrowed. "Aside from several whining about this vote, that you—a sophisticated, young woman—frequented a questionable place. Good deeds do not always reflect wise decision-making."

She bent over in her chair. Bile bubbled up from her throat. "Were all the readers upset?"

"Not all the letters were damning. I will admit a few indicated your bravery was commendable."

She straightened up and placed her hands together under her chin. "That is a small victory, don't you think so?"

"You cannot keep writing about controversial subjects. Our readers will stop buying our paper and pick up the *City Sun Times*."

"We have scores of women readers. Why would you not think they will remain loyal?"

"Do you believe your support of the vote has captured our women readers?"

"I do. The ladies I have spoken to at society luncheons also want the vote."

Her father shook his head. "I don't know. It's a gamble."

Her heart pounded in her ears. "Please, Papa, how can I convince you to approve? I will not be in danger in those old clothes."

"Listen to me, my ambitious daughter. Today's rally is not fresh news. The fight for the vote is half a century old, and nothing has changed. Do you understand?"

"Women keep fighting despite the failures. Don't you find that worthwhile?"

He stood and crossed his arms over his chest. "No. Women's rights are a hopeless cause to pursue."

"It's a problem, Papa. Women have no choice. They stay home—raise the children, crochet, and gossip. They should be able to choose, even if they prefer to stay home and gossip."

"If they don't run the house and raise the children, who will?"

"Voting and freedom of choice are the requests. Do you think women will forego their responsibilities?"

Allie refused to back down. Disobedience to her father crushed her spirit. The fight was not with her father but with her father's obligation, as publisher of his newspaper, *The New York Sentinel,* to inform and support women. She had to convince him to agree. The excitement and enthusiasm for her column could increase the readership, but his worry about losing readers pushed him into a corner. He worried more about money than women's rights. Her heart cried out. She had a voice. But it was her voice he wanted to silence.

"The women will continue to raise the children and keep house." Allie bit her lip, trying to hold back the tears and keep her lips from trembling.

Joseph shook his head. "I cannot give you permission to write about these sensitive political issues."

"You have inspired me to be a writer, to tell the truth, to be diverse. Why not give me the freedom to write this column? My column offers women respect and acknowledges their intelligence."

He leaned forward and twisted his lips. "Your safety is vital."

"It's a public event. There will be patrolmen there."

"Your writing will bring unrest."

"Why?"

"Enough!" Her father's hand came down hard on his desk, the letters fluttering to the floor.

Allie jerked to her feet, sending her chair flying backward. It hit the wall across from his desk with a satisfying bang. "If Adam were sitting here instead of me, this would not be a discussion." Her voice was loud enough to wake the family. She fixed her hand over her mouth. A tear escaped. She always enjoyed her father's library, but not today. Now the deep wine colors seemed morbid, and the touches of green and gold from his porcelain collection felt gauche and pretentious.

"For heaven's sake, your brother has nothing to do with this. Maybe it will be different in fifty years, but right now, I don't want another caper, and I don't want another stack of letters complaining about you." He hesitated for a long moment. "I don't want you putting yourself at risk. I will not publish your rally articles. We'll see about going to this event. I'll talk it over with your mother. Maybe take Mia along to keep you out of trouble."

Allie should not have to get consent for anything, especially not attending the rally. After all, at twenty-three and not a child, she wanted to be a serious journalist, at a serious paper, covering serious news. Instead, she was still writing about another wedding, another birth, another engagement, and wasting time answering readers' inquiries to the "Dear Miss Demeanor's" advice column.

Why must I ask for permission?

She plucked at her dress, her muscles quivering. Her father pulled a handkerchief from his coat pocket and handed it to her. She dried her tears.

She put her arms around him and planted a kiss on his cheek. "I'm sure you know that you have taught me to be courageous and stand up for what I believe."

He gave her a kiss that tickled and made her giggle.

"And you know that I only want the best for you. I'm proud of you despite your antics."

Darn him.

"Regardless, Papa, I will get those interviews . . ." she said, turning away with "today" on her lips. She closed the door, leaving the harsh words behind her, and marched down the hallway to get some breakfast.

It was late, and she had to get to the rally. Allie stopped in the kitchen for a cup of coffee and one of Mrs. Bigelow's baked muffins cooling on the counter. She wrapped one in a napkin, took a few sips of coffee, and ran past the library. The carpeted stairs silenced her footsteps as she ran to her bedroom.

Allie took a bite of the soft cinnamon muffin topped with crunchy, buttery crumbs. Captyn, her black-and-white Great Dane, sidled up to her. She patted his smooth, furry head. "This is too sugary for you, and I can't play now. I'm off to do my duty. Shhh. No barking."

She pulled her carpetbag out from the back of her wardrobe and changed into a long, brown day dress and a bulky, tattered coat that hid her slender frame. She tucked her curls under a floppy hat, stuffed her feet into scruffy boots, and tied the laces while Captyn licked the back of her hand.

"Captyn, stop that." She wiped the back of her hand on the old coat, picked up the bag with its three bocce balls sewed into the lining for protection, and hefted it over her shoulder. Taking her unfinished muffin and closing the door behind her, she ran past her sister's bedroom and down the back stairs to the hallway. She darted into the courtyard where the gardener worked with the fall plantings, filling the garden with the warm colors of orange and yellow chrysanthemums. "Morning, Miss Allie."

"Good morning," Allie said in a cheery tone. *Uh-oh. He recognized me hiding under this hat.*

She opened the gate, ran to the line of carriages waiting for a fare, and beckoned the nearest buggy.

ON A SUNNY, BRISK AUTUMN DAY, HUNDREDS OF PEOPLE surrounded New York City Hall, where Presidents Lincoln and Grant lay in state the year before. The building became a symbol for Peter—the touchstone to life as a boy of eleven when he went to work with his father. The flags and the thousands with their tears viewing the past presidents remained in his heart.

This day, the crowds stood shoulder to shoulder, filling the streets and gardens across the way. Hundreds of women and men assembled for the women's rally. Many carried signs with the word *VOTE*. A few eggs thrown at the display signs by those who opposed the rally partially obliterated the inked letters.

In his spiffy checked trousers, Peter Harrison did not see the missile coming as he stood guard on the hall's steps. Raw, rotten egg coated his forehead and dripped down his face onto his high-buttoned, grey sack coat, perfectly clean and tailored not too many minutes ago. His stomach retched at the awful smell he would have to tolerate all day. He yanked a handkerchief out of his pocket and wiped off the dirty, sticky mess.

"Where are you, you sneaky bastards?" Peter mumbled.

The culprits blended in with the spectators. Peter spotted more eggs hurtling over the crowd, splattering on the steps and knocking off hats. When the miscreants moved closer, Peter's six-foot-four frame allowed him to observe two youths battling a woman. Zigzagging his way past clusters of listeners, his face tight and his eyes keen, he prepared to confront the criminals.

"Stand back, stand back. Let me through." Peter, now stuck in the thick of the crowd, spied the two stocky youths reaching for eggs piled high in two buckets on the cobblestone street. A woman, engulfed in a tattered coat, shouted, "Stop it!" Her dark blue hat flopped as she grunted, hefting an oversized carpetbag and swinging it at the head of the taller youth.

The Women's Social Reform Society had hired the Harrison Detective Agency to keep order at the rally. Damned if he'd let a cantankerous old woman and two oversized youths ruin the peace at one of his events. Peter pushed through the crowd to get to the troublesome trio. He grinned at the sight of the old woman. Who was this person trying to be an enforcer for the beleaguered ladies on the podium?

The old woman swung her bag at the youths again. "How dare you bully those women!"

The boys leaned back, avoiding the swing, and snorted with laughter. She gawked and wound up for another go. After another swing and a miss, the bag made a strange thumping sound, like a croquet mallet hitting a ball through a wicket, as it moved through the air.

"Lady, you look funny," the taller of the two crowed.

"You find me funny? I'll give you funny." She took a deep breath and tightened her hold on the handles, then whirled the bag in a wide arc, missing the shorter youth by a hair's breadth.

"Look out, Jeb," he shouted.

She clipped the older one on the shoulder.

"Ouch! Ya could've given me more warning, Ed." Jeb rubbed the sore spot and glared at the woman.

The woman stood with her feet shoulder-width

apart, sporting a pair of brown galoshes that looked like they'd slogged across Ireland and back.

"What's your problem? We ain't got no beef with you," Ed echoed.

Jeb lobbed two more eggs at the stage and knocked off a speaker's plumed hat.

Before the woman could swing her flowered bag again, Jeb grabbed ahold of it, but her steely grip on the handle triggered a tug-of-war. People came alongside to help. A sturdy woman in a baker's apron reached for the purse to help while an older man sporting a porkpie hat joined Jeb's side. A football cheer went up for their favorite, the boys or the woman. "Rah, Rah, S-s-s-t! Boom! Ah-hh!"

With no other choice, Peter dug into his pants' pocket for his whistle and blew it three times to signal his men stationed around the perimeter. Everyone froze. The bag thumped on the cobblestones and lay there. Two of Peter's best men, O'Malley and Spencer, arrived from opposite directions and grabbed the brothers by their collars.

"Dang," Ed said. "Let go. We ain't done nothin' wrong. Just tryin' to get those wacky women to shut up."

"Throwing eggs and shouting insults is wrong!" Peter thundered as he reached the boys, grabbing the bucket of eggs at their feet.

Jeb shook his fist at Peter. "You ain't got no right to steal 'r eggs."

They both earned a slap on their ears from his men.

"Take these young men to the station. Captain O'Sullivan can remind them about proper behavior and notify their parents," Peter ordered.

Ed and Jeb continued to squawk as Peter's men dragged them away.

"Hey, why did you take those boys away?" the porkpie-hat man yelled.

"Having some harmless fun," another joined in.

"Throwing eggs at women is not harmless fun," the apron lady declared.

"Trash is what they are," a man bellowed from the crowd.

"The boys belong in jail!" hollered another.

Peter's hackles rose as the people traded angry barbs.

He addressed the woman with the carpetbag. "Ma'am, there's trouble brewing from your interference. I cannot trust you. You are going to have to come with me to the guest tent to calm down."

"I will do no such thing." The old woman yanked her hat downward. "If you don't mind, I will stay right here and listen to the rest of the speeches."

Her voice sounded loud for an old woman.

"Ma'am." Peter offered the crook of his arm. "Permit

me to escort you to the tent where you can have a cup of tea and collect yourself. Then you may return to hear the women speakers."

"I am not moving."

A screech of wagon wheels sounded down the street. Peter's eyes narrowed. A mob of men and women climbed down from a wagon and rushed into the excited crowd. "Stop the vote! Stop the vote!"

"Damn! Rabble-rousers," Peter projected.

Three short whistles from Peter and his men launched into action again. The old woman could be trouble in the burgeoning melee. Scooping her into his arms, he strode to the tent, taking her out of the commotion.

"Unhand me!" she yelled.

"Just keeping you from making more trouble, ma'am."

She pointed at him. "I am not the troublemaker here."

He moved straight away, not paying attention to her or her squirming. "Must you shriek in my ear?" he asked in a stern tone.

"I wanted to be sure you heard me."

"I heard you fine, and I'm not unhanding you."

She sucked in a big breath. "Put me down, or I'll scream in your ear again."

"Ma'am, I'm sure you had good intentions to stop those boys, but your actions added to the commotion."

Peter tightened his hold and hauled her to a tented area on the side of the building. The woman squirmed like a monkey in a barrel of eels.

"You have nerve. Who do you think you are, anyway? Put me down this instant."

Peter tried to keep his balance and maintain his hold.

"I can't do that, ma'am. You can either calm down here or in a jail cell," Peter said in a biting tone while looking straight ahead. He leaned his head left and then right, trying to see around the woman's confounded hat, realizing too late when his booted foot tripped on one of the thick ropes on the ground securing the tent.

"My hat!"

"Oomph!" Peter toppled over, twisting his large frame to cushion the woman's body. Unfortunately, it also meant taking the brunt of the fall. His bowler went flying.

They landed with a bone-jarring thud.

The old woman yelped.

Peter groaned and shifted on the hard-packed earth. Still clutching the woman, he winced and shook his head to clear his vision.

His breath caught at the sight in his arms. He stared

at an oval face with high cheekbones, a sprinkling of freckles decorating a pert nose, and a tumble of enchanting red curls.

Peter straightened the spectacles on her nose. With the magnificent, impish creature sprawled atop him, the commotion behind him faded away.

He knitted his brows. "You are no old lady."

"I never said I was," she said, her words clipped.

"Miss, I believe we need to alter our positions." Peter smoothly lifted her off his body, scrambled to his feet, and helped her up.

"Heavens." The young woman wobbled in her clunky galoshes, and her hands flew to her wild curls.

"My hat," she whined in a loud voice.

Spotting the monstrosity dangling from a tent pole, Peter reached up and unhooked it. He turned it over as if seeking an identifying mark and regarded her with a teasing gaze.

The woman stared back at him. A rueful smile curved her lips. She cocked her head. "Sir, will you please return my hat?" she asked in a sweet voice while her eyes shot daggers at him.

He almost grinned. Almost. There was something irresistible about the woman, a coquettish feminism he'd never encountered before. The women he'd met were anything but flirty. They were rather serious ladies with an unrelenting passion for seeing this rally succeed. How he ever mistook her for an elderly matron was beyond him. Her youthfulness was apparent not only in her actions but in her beauty. It was the old, tattered clothing that made him assume her age matched her appearance.

"My hat if you please."

"Not until you answer my question," he said, his voice mellow. "Why did you wear these unlikely clothes?" he asked, trying to ignore how the lady's freckles made her look like a naughty imp.

She planted both hands squarely on her hips. At least he thought they were her hips under that bulky coat.

"Did no one teach you it's rude to be blunt?"

"You were engaged in a public altercation, placing yourself and others at risk."

Her smirk changed into a regal smile. "I did no such thing."

Peter waved the hat in front of her pert nose. "Then explain."

She shrugged. "I dressed for inclement weather. Besides, what I am wearing is none of your business. Those thugs needed a lesson. I did well on my own, thank you."

"You think so, do you?" He cracked a smile at her antics.

"I will take my hat if you don't mind." She snatched

it from his hands, yanked it down on her head, and tied the strings under her stubborn chin.

Peter could not resist teasing her. "Did you get those boots to muck about in a barn?"

"Harrison," a voice said, booming from down the street.

Allie crossed her arms and glared at the man. "I will have you know these boots are the latest, most fashionable, finest nubuck leather."

He looked down his nose at her, enjoying their banter. "Your fancy boots can't save you, and you could be in a bit of trouble."

She glared at him. "What kind of trouble?"

"Wait in the tent, or I'll arrest you on charges of disorderly conduct and disturbing the peace," Peter said over his shoulder, grabbing his hat from the ground as he rushed away.

I HOPE YOU ENJOYED THIS FREE PREVIEW OF *THE Unforgettable Miss Baldwin*, Book 2 in The American Heiresses Series. Each novel in the series is a stand-alone story and can be read in any order—though they're especially delightful when enjoyed in sequence.

If you'd like to keep reading *for free* with Kindle Unlimited, simply click or scan the QR code below.

ABOUT THE AUTHOR

Brooklyn-born Gail Ingis, author of **THE AMERICAN HEIRESSES** series, will whisk you away into the whirlwind worlds of historical romance. And just when you think you know her, she surprises readers with her memoir, *More Than One Life*, proving she has more twists than a double helix. Gail firmly believes that everyone's life is a novel waiting to be written—and that a chance encounter with a stranger is often just the prelude to the next captivating chapter.

But wait—there's more! Gail isn't just a wordsmith; she's also an award-winning artist whose paintings have appeared in *The New York Times* and other publications.

She serves as an art juror, helping curate creativity at the celebrated **Lockwood Mathews Mansion Museum,** in Norwalk, Connecticut—voted one of *USA*

Today's top 10 museums in America—where she wears many hats, including trustee and art curator.

In addition to wielding both pen and paintbrush, Gail held a tennis racquet for many years as a proud member in the RSPA (**Racquet Sports Professionals Association**), formerly the USPTA (United States Professional Tennis Association), Gail's interests are as varied as a buffet at a Vegas casino—rich, diverse, and delightfully indulgent.

A retired member of the American Society of Interior Designers (ASID), Gail added "founder" to her already bulging résumé in 1981 by establishing the Interior Design Institute (IDI), which later merged with Berkeley College. Her teaching adventures took her to the New York School of Interior Design (NYSID) and other prestigious universities throughout the New York tri-state area, where she shared her wisdom—and her wit.

These days, Gail calls Connecticut home, where she and her dashing husband, Tom, are living their best lives. Their days include tennis matches, gardening sessions, Beatrix Potter children's book marathons, popular writers' fiction, and epic Costco adventures— always capped off with a legendary $1.50 hot dog and diet soda. Together, they've raised five wonderful children, seventeen grandchildren (including four spouses), and three great-grandchildren—and rumor has it the family tree is still sprouting new branches.

Gail loves hearing from readers. You can message her through her website at **gailingis.com**, where you'll find details about her books, a gallery of her paintings, and access to her blog archive containing over 500 articles covering everything from books to ballroom dancing.

Follow Gail on social media at one or more of the platforms below:

BOOKS BY GAIL INGIS

Fiction

THE AMERICAN HEIRESSES SERIES

The Memorable Mrs. Dempsey

The Unforgettable Miss Baldwin

A Match for Mischief

Non-Fiction

More Than One Life ~ A Memoir